NORTH WITH DOC

The In-Fisherman Library Series

Greg Knowles

Published by In-Fisherman Inc.

IN-FISHERMAN CORPORATE BOOK DIVISION

Director *Al Lindner*
Publisher Emeritus *Ron Lindner*
Chief Executive Officer *Dave Lauer*
Chief Operations Officer *Dan Sura*
Publisher *Stewart Legaard*
Editor In Chief *Doug Stange*

NORTH WITH DOC

Written by *Greg Knowles*
Illustrated by *Peter Kohlsaat*
Edited by *Doug Stange* and *Joann Phipps*
Cover Design and Art Direction by *Chuck Nelson,*
 Nelson Graphic Design
Design and Layout by *James Pfaff*
Litho Prep by *Quality Graphics*
Printing by *Bang Printing*

ISBN 0-929384-40-7

The In-Fisherman® Library Series

An
F (Fish) + L (Location) + P (Presentation) = S (Success)™
Educational Service

Published by In-Fisherman® Inc., Two
In-Fisherman Dr., Brainerd, MN 56401. Text and
illustrations copyrighted 1993 by In-Fisherman Inc.
Rights reserved.
No part of this book may be reproduced or
transmitted in any form or by any means, electronic
or mechanical, including photocopying, recording,
or by any information storage and retrieval system
without written permission from the Editor In Chief.

First Edition, 1993
Second Printing, 1995

As most often happens when characters are created in a series of stories, a start-up period exists in which the author builds a relationship with his main character. It was as if, in this case, Doc's feelings would be hurt if not treated with utmost respect. But after a few episodes, as I became more acquainted with Doc, I discovered the cigar smoking dentist-fisherman was not only fallible, but sometimes completely out of touch with reality. In other words, Doc (and friends) became human.

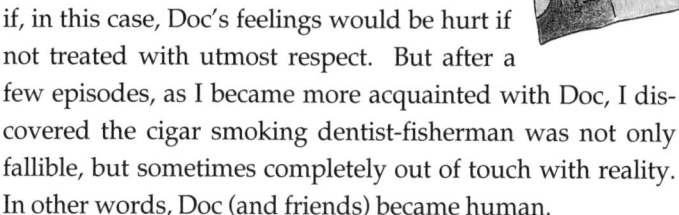

This, though, is a work of fiction. Any resemblance between Doc and his friends and any of my friends is coincidental. Knobby Clark's Sioux Lookout fly-in business, the Northwest Ontario lakes, and the fishing they offer are, however, very real.

Anyone who has fished with friends, whether on an Iowa farm pond or on some faraway excursion to the Canadian Bush, should see himself in these episodes. Unmistakable too is an appreciation of nature, the excitement of a fish on the line, some questionable advice, and, I hope, a few smiles along the way.

I owe thanks to In-Fisherman Editor-In-Chief Doug Stange and Managing Editor Joann Phipps for their support and work in putting this book together. And a big tip o' the word processor to Peter Kohlsaat for the crafty caricatures that bring Doc and friends to life.

I hope you enjoy reading about Doc as much as I enjoy writing about him.

Greg Knowles

TABLE OF CONTENTS

EPISODE	PAGE
1. LOOKING GOOD MEANS FEELING GOOD MEANS CATCHING MORE FISH	7
2. IT ONLY COSTS A LITTLE LESS TO GO WORST CLASS	11
3. WHERE PIKE FLY HIGH	15
4. IF YOU GET LOST IN THE WILDERNESS, IT'S GOOD TO HAVE A FRIEND ALONG	19
5. WHAT TO DO WHEN THE FISH STOP BITING AND THE FISHERMEN START	25
6. TAKING THE FAMILY CAR ON A FISHING TRIP IS DRIVING A HARD BARGAIN	31
7. FRIENDS, SNORERS, AND FISHERMEN LEND ME YOUR EARS	37
8. IF YOU LET A SMILE BE YOUR UMBRELLA, YOU'LL BE ONE MISERABLE FISHERMAN	43
9. WITH THE OUTBOARD IN GEAR, THE BRAIN MUST NOT BE IN NEUTRAL	49
10. A SHARP HOOK MEETING A DULL MIND CAN BE A BLOODY SHAME	55
11. EVERY NOW AND THEN, A FISHERMAN NEEDS A TUNE-UP	61
12. FEW WIVES WHO REFUSE TO BAIT A HOOK WILLINGLY SANCTION A STAG FISHING TRIP	67
13. WALLEYES AREN'T ALWAYS GREENER ON THE OTHER SIDE OF THE RAPIDS	75

14. BUSH HOG BUFFET 85

15. BRAIN BACKLASH 93

16. IF A PICTURE'S WORTH 1,000 WORDS,
    I HAVE A LIBRARY IN MY CLOSET 99

17. WHERE THERE'S SMOKING
    THERE'S FIRE 107

18. WHEN DADS AND KIDS GO SEPARATE WAYS
    IT USUALLY WORKS OUT IN THE END 115

19. SOMETIMES MEMORIES MAKE
    BETTER TROPHIES 123

20. EVEN AN ECOSLOB CAN
    CLEAN UP HIS ACT 131

21. SOMETIMES THE NORTHWEST ONTARIO
    BUSH CAN BE COLDER THAN AUNT LUCY'S
    GREEN BEAN CASSEROLE 139

22. NIGHTMARE ON WALLEYE STREET 147

23. FOR SOME FISHERMEN, TROLLING IS
    THE END OF THE LINE 153

24. A FISH IN THE NET IS WORTH
    TWO IN THE LAKE 159

25. POTTY TALK 165

EPISODE 1

Looking Good Means Feeling Good Means Catching More Fish

For years, I've joined the guys to fish Northwest Ontario for a week in early June, the best time there for fish quality and quantity. It's also an unpredictable time, however, for weather and insects, two wet blankets of fishing.

I remember my fishing companions laughing aloud at what I'd packed for our annual trip—waterproof boots, with the sky clear to the horizon. But two days later when rain turned our boats into wading pools, I was high on being dry.

The guys busted a gut at my beekeeper headgear. But when black flies swarmed and mosquitoes burrowed into their ears, their arms and poles flailed the air like copter rotors while I hummed a happy tune and kept on fishing.

After a few years of seeing my preparedness pay off, the other guys in the group followed suit, so to speak. Soon we all owned the boots, hats, rain suits, gloves, electric socks, and other apparel that add some creature comforts while fishing the Canadian Bush.

One year, we had a last minute cancellation, so I invited my dentist, a self-professed expert angler, to join the fun. I called him Doc when he wasn't beating me at cutthroat pitch, and Doc managed to teach us all a thing or two about what a successful fisherman wears.

June 9th. Our Ojibway pilot, who looked to be about 14, flew six of us plus all our gear and provisions out of Sioux Lookout, Ontario. The flight improved above the 500-foot ceiling. Luckily the clouds broke enough an hour later for the pilot to land the ancient de Havilland at our remote outpost. Then the weather fell apart.

Donning rain suits and boots, we unloaded in the downpour, carrying provisions up a mudslick hill to the only cabin on the lake. As the plane taxied out, the rain stopped and snow fell. We started a fire and looked out the windows at a summertime mini-blizzard dusting the boats.

While the rest of us argued over whether to break out the Oreos or the dry-roasted peanuts, Doc unpacked his wardrobe. Our standard baggage for the one-week stay in the Bush included a Navy sea bag or large duffel for clothes and a small gym bag for toiletries. Doc's baggage was not standard. Besides the large duffel and gym bag, he had a huge suitcase. As we munched our Oreos and peanuts, we wandered over to see what he'd brought.

Out of the large duffel emerged light and heavy jackets, light and heavy gloves, winter and summer hats, three sets of long underwear, an Iowa Hawkeye sweatshirt, two bathing suits, four bath towels, two washcloths, two sets of bed sheets, a pillow, a blanket, and two pillowcases, all wrapped in plastic. He piled all this on an extra bunk.

Next came the underwear and socks, each set in its own plastic bag labeled DAY 1, DAY 2 . . . Other bags were labeled EXTRA HOT, EXTRA COLD, and EXTRA WET. Doc explained that these were for weather extremes when a fisherman might want to change clothes more than once a day. This brought hoo-haws from a couple guys. As for me, though, feelings of inadequacy welled up in my gizzard, pancreas, or whatever organ is south of my belly button where butterflies occasionally flutter.

Then Doc unzipped the huge suitcase. Shirts and pants hung on plastic hangers. He stretched a nylon rope between a couple nails and began hanging them up. Seven pairs of casual slacks, various colors with matching belts of fabric and leather threaded through the loops. No jeans or work pants in sight.

His shirts were button-down-collar oxfords with a few chamois thrown in for good measure. If our fillet knives got dull, we could use the creases in Doc's shirt sleeves to clean the fish.

Now, we all like being clean and maybe even neat while languishing in a fisherman's paradise without electricity and bathing or laundry facilities. And while a few borderline slobs in the group would wear a pair of northern-slimed jeans for two days in a row, we all changed underwear and socks daily. But this display of toggery was too much. I shuffled over to my bunk and surveyed my adequate, but disheveled accoutrements packed randomly in Hefty's best and stuffed in my sea bag.

If our fillet knives got dull, we could use the creases in Doc's shirt sleeves to clean the fish.

"Doc, why all the fancy duds?"

"When I look good, I feel good," he replied. "And when I feel good, I believe a positive aura surrounds me and I catch more and bigger fish." As we choked on our Oreos, we decided we didn't know Doc well enough yet to ridicule him further, so we let it go.

"But what about the grime and fishstink?" I asked.

"That's what washing machines are for," Doc said. And I had to agree. But we'd come to fish. So, crummy weather or no, we rigged our rods and suited up. The thrill of the first few walleyes kept temperatures high under watertight jackets and pants, and we were all well prepared for the sleet that began peppering us.

I watched awestruck as Doc, who was my boat partner, boated twice the fish I did. Most appeared just a little bigger than mine, too. We were using the same line, same jig weight, and same color plastic tail. I even mimicked his jigging motion with my identical rod. Nothing helped.

As daylight dimmed, we motored to shore and cleaned a dozen dinner-bound walleyes. Inside the warm cabin, after peeling off our foul weather gear, everyone stood in sweaty jeans and wrinkled flannel shirts. Everyone except Doc.

Watching him strip his rain gear, I was reminded of an early James Bond movie, the one where 007 comes out of the ocean in a wet suit, unzips and steps onto the beach in a tux. The only difference between Bond and Doc was the absence of a flower in Doc's lapel. His shirt collar stood up like a Marine's and his pants were creased, the cuffs rustling as he rolled them up and headed for the stove.

That week, Doc won all the contests for biggest and most fish, as well as "Best Dressed In the Bush." He even turned out to be a pretty good cook. And even though I lost a car payment to him at the pitch table, the week still ranked high as one of the best times I've ever had.

Although jeans are my favorite pants and I don't care much for starch in my shirts, I've decided it doesn't hurt to have them pressed and fresh when I climb into the boat. After all, feeling good about one's appearance is important in attracting the opposite sex, so why not apply it to fishing?

Since that time, some 20 seasons ago, Doc has always joined us on our trips. And each time, the rest of us dress a little more carefully. And we catch a few more and a few bigger fish.

Thanks, Doc.

EPISODE 2

It Only Costs A Little Less To Go Worst Class

Seems a lifetime ago that a friend of a friend called and invited me to fill out a Canadian fishing party of six. I'd seen the pictures and heard the tales they brought back from Northwest Ontario. They spoke dreamily of a single primitive cabin, no electricity or running water, a remote lake. And although a week of fishing, food, and refreshment figured to a then staggering tab of about $300, I decided it was time to take the plunge.

The first weekend in June, we stepped from a de Havilland float plane onto the dock at a lake about 90 miles north of Sioux Lookout. As advertised, the experience was like none other. The fishing was everything I'd hoped for, and the camaraderie was exceptional.

One small deficiency, however. While planning the provisions list, we decided to save money on food and other necessities by buying generic. Generic cooking oil, generic dish soap, generic condiments, generic pancake flour, generic peanut butter, generic canned bacon, and generic paper products. Matter of fact, the only items not generic were the lettuce, eggs, onions, and potatoes. And on second thought, I'm not so sure about the eggs.

I'd been led to believe that generic items have to meet the same government dictated requirements as brand names. But somewhere along the way, quality took it on the chin. I mean, why do you suppose brand name stuff costs more? Could be the fancy packaging that drives prices up, but I think the main reason is better quality. Sure, generic salt and pepper, matches, and a few canned goods are close to brand name caliber, but they're just not the same as the real McCoy.

So there we were in the Canadian wilds, stacking food on three wimpy generic paper plates instead of one; soaking up rivers of grease from generic canned bacon with an extra four sheets of generic paper toweling; adding generic ketchup to generic pork and beans to make them palatable; gagging down generic canned peaches; and spreading generic peanut butter on generic bread that tasted like generic cardboard. And speaking of cardboard, let's not forget the generic toilet paper. Yowch!

But boy did we save money! We calculated that buying generic for the six-man party had cut about $45 from the total bill for the week. Hmmm. Forty-five divided by six is $7.50. So for six days in the Bush, each of us had saved about, umm, let's see . . . $1.25 a day. (At that time, $1.25 would have bought three gallons of gas or a couple packs of cheap cigars or a burger and fries and a soda pop at the local fast fooderie.)

Six days later when the plane took off to return us to civilization, however, a couple boxes of black-and-white packaged goods were left behind. Nobody wanted to take them home.

We were way too lazy to change for the better, so we continued the generic tradition for a number of years . . . until Doc joined the group. Since Doc was a relative rookie, he was volunteered to supply transportation. We gave him some static about his Cadillac, and he blamed it on his being a small town dentist with an image to maintain. But it was light-years better than the VW bus I drove the year before, so those of us lucky enough to ride with Doc didn't mind a bit.

To avoid delays at the border and to escape from duty payments on our groceries, we shopped at a Canadian supermarket for supplies. We trooped into the store, bent on adhering to the list and getting back on the road to catch the flight out. But Doc proved to be a problem.

Each time anyone placed a generic product in the cart, Doc replaced it with a brand name item. Out went the generic chocolate cookies with white filling, in came the Oreos. Out went the imitation maple syrup, in came Aunt Jemima. Out went the pasteurized process cheese spread, and in came the Kraft cheddar. Tempers began to flare somewhere between the generic tartar sauce and the generic lemon juice.

As a neophyte, Doc was chastised for trying to take control of provisions. I'll have to admit that I put in my two cents worth. To end the discussion, Doc volunteered to make up out of his own pocket any difference in the cost of generic versus brand name products. (I should mention here that nobody in the group was destitute. As a matter of fact, we were all gainfully employed. It was just the principle of the thing. But we decided if Doc wanted to throw his money away, fine.)

It took an extra 20 minutes to do the shopping, because for comparison purposes we had to write down prices on generic items we didn't buy. Imagine our surprise when the total difference came to a whopping $24.30! An almost unbearable financial burden of $4.05 per man. And we let Doc have it heavy until a couple days later when what he'd accomplished began to sink in.

Our turnaround opinion of Doc was gradual, but our week in the Bush ended as an unqualified success. The fishing was superb, the company was beyond reproach, and the food was not generic.

At each meal, we gave thanks for the brand name products. The peanut butter and pickles and potato chips tasted better than ever. The salad dressings and cookies were bright spots on the menu. The fish tasted even better served on sturdy paper plates. And the Charmin was (Ahh!) just plain charming.

And the Charmin was (Ahh!) just plain charming.

We unanimously released Doc from his pledge to subsidize the food bill, and we each in our own way praised his determination to add a little more flavor to the trip. The next year saw hamburgers providing variety to the twice-a-day fish fare. And as the years went by and the outfitter added gas refrigerators and ovens to his outposts, we flew in with milk, sausages, steaks, chicken, more fresh vegetables, and even frozen pies to bake.

As we look back to earlier trips, we wonder how we ever managed to get by without Doc. Or without having spaghetti at least one night during our stay. Or a nice glass of Valpolicella with a plate of walleye Florentine. Or hors d'oeuvres of sweet pickles, cheddar chunks, and summer sausage on wheat crackers as a preface to stuffed peppers.

And through all this classy cuisine, the lakes stay just as clean, the air just as fresh, and my appreciation for fishing and friendship just keeps on growing.

Thanks, Doc.

EPISODE 3

Where Pike Fly High

Some years ago, six of us boarded a familiar float plane and flew due north out of Sioux Lookout, Ontario, with our hopes high and our airsick bags at the ready. The 50-year-old de Havilland performed like a 50-year-old de Havilland, and an hour and a half later we set up residence in the only cabin on an incredibly scenic, pristine Canadian lake. The loons were looning and the grouse were grousing as we paired up in three boats, setting out to catch dinner.

I've wetted lines in lots of places, but early June in the Canadian Bush is about as close to ideal as I've ever come. As we motored away from shore, a dozen shades of greenery merged into a soothing forested blur, camouflaging bays and islands. And after a couple hundred yards, even the bright red cabin disappeared. The wake of dark water imprisoned in solid ice a little more than a month before frothed cleanly behind us.

The bouquet of burned boat gas gives me goose bumps on any body of water. But mingled with the northern air, it's a veritable olfactory orgy. As I felt my first northern pike slam my lure, I knew this would be the continuation of a 20-year string of outstanding Canadian outings.

Northerns are mighty mean fish—even the smaller ones are fun to catch on light tackle—but they're also fragile. That's why we always try to crank them in fast and release them while they still have a lot of fight and a lot of life left in them.

As is our habit, we trolled spoons for northerns until our heartbeats slowed and we could settle down to a serious walleye drift and jig. We'd caught and released a dozen or so snakes when all at once WHAM! and "Get the net!" from Doc, my boat partner. He had what looked to be a decent fish on his line.

"Trampoline it!" Doc yelled.

"Do what?" I said.

And Doc screamed, "Trampoline it!" with a "fishcaught" fire in his eyes and his new light-action number doing a dance toward the down side of the lake. Since I was a stranger to this trampoline talk, I scooped up the northern on the second run and brought it on board.

Ever seen a fish with real sharp teeth, fins, and gill covers do a pirouette in a net? If you've netted a northern pike, you have. And if you've ever unwrapped one of those slimy seven-pounders from its nylon mummy, you know what a chunk it can take out of your fishing time. Your fingers, too, if you're not careful.

Back then, I'd known Doc for only a short time. Mostly, we'd stared at each other over a hand or two of pitch or cribbage, or he'd carried on a one-sided conversation while both of his hands were in my mouth. Did I mention Doc's my dentist? Well, he is. A pretty good one, I guess, because

I still have most of my teeth. And he's a pretty good fisherman, too.

But at that point, Doc was not at all pleased as he began sorting out about a thousand fish teeth and five hooks on his Ruby-Eye that were spun into a major league mess in the net. (The unwritten rule of boat partners: It's his fish, so it's his mess.) He gave me a disappointed look as a light breeze took the boat along a magnificent rock wall and I jigged for walleyes.

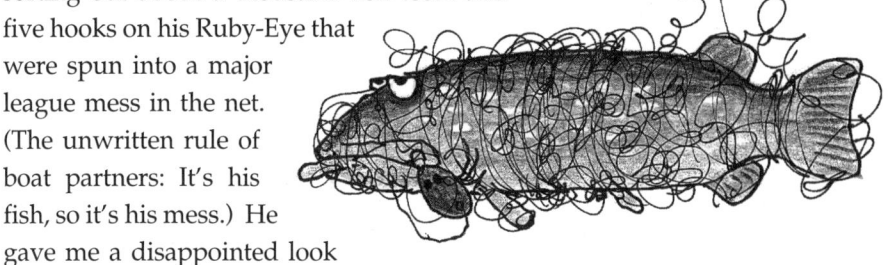

After I'd put a couple eaters on the stringer, Doc gave out a sigh. He was ready to fish again. Just as soon as he offered advice about proper use of the net.

First he showed me the northern. It took so long to free the beast that it had to go on the dinner table instead of back in the drink.

Second, he said it looked like we'd drifted through a walleye honey hole, and if he hadn't been fooling with the tangle, he could have helped fill the stringer.

Third, it's okay to deep net a trophy northern, but nothing in the 12-pound-or-under range. And if I do it again, he'll make it up to me the next time I'm in for a checkup. I stopped jigging and began listening.

"Here's how to trampoline a fish," Doc said, as he picked up the net. "You grab hold of the net material like this." He grabbed the net material. "And you pull it tight." He pulled it tight. "You see, instead of a deep dish, that makes a flat surface, like a trampoline. Then, you shove it under the fish and kind of bounce him out of the water."

Hmmm. This had possibilities. No teeth or hooks in the net. No tangles. No wasted time. Less chance of injuring the fish. I'd give it a try. I experimented on a few small walleyes and the technique seemed workable. Now for the acid test.

Doc had a three-pound axe-handle northern hooked. I grabbed the net, bunched the nylon material, pulled it tight, shoved it under the fish, and boooinng! It flew completely over the boat.

On the second try, I tossed the critter about eight feet into the air where he spit the hook, did a two-and-a-half (in pike position) and was off like a shot when he hit the water. I managed to get the next fish into the boat, but it landed in an open tackle box. Mine. Doc was amused.

Bass and bluegill and crappie fishermen may find trampoline netting downright distasteful. After all, with a thumb and a few fingers, it's relatively easy to yank almost any size toothless species right out of the water. And sportsmen who fish for northern pike with professional regularity (more than once a year, usually on TV) have probably mastered the art of snatching 20-pounders under the gill covers and dragging them on board without damaging fish or fingers. I figure the first time I try that, I'll never play the violin again. So I think I'll stick with Doc's trick until something better comes along.

I'll be the first to admit it took a little practice to get the hang of trampoline netting. But after several dozen successes, I had it mastered. On subsequent fishing trips, my less worldly companions have marveled at my expertise with no-hassle fish landing. But being the unselfish sportsman I am, I gladly give credit where credit's due.

Thanks, Doc.

EPISODE 4

If You Get Lost In The Wilderness, It's Good To Have A Friend Along

June 1st about 15 years ago, six seasoned fishermen boarded an antique but freshly refinished de Havilland float plane, bound for the Canadian Bush. From Sioux Lookout, the flight was a little over an hour due north.

We fished a different lake each year, and Knobby, our outfitter, made sure we had detailed maps. He even marked where our one-and-only cabin on the lake was located, as well as the best spots for walleyes and northern pike. No guides were available, and although hundreds of Ojibway Indians lived in the area, they were rarely seen.

> *He was used to standing in one place all day, jigging twenty-dollar bills out of patients' mouths.*

We make our annual trip to Canada because the scenery is as spectacular as the fishing. And the colors, well, the next time you're in a paint store, check the color selection guide. The greens from dark to more subtle hues paint Northwest Ontario from late May through early September. Pines, birch, bushes, and reeds blend to form a continuous shoreline. But as you motor closer, dozens of camouflaged inlets, bays, and islands appear.

We arrived late in the afternoon the first day, so we fished a fast-water narrows within sight of the cabin. The second day, Doc and I were boat partners. We headed south, while the other two boats headed north. We'd packed a lunch, two six-packs, and plenty of cigars for an all-dayer.

As we trolled over weedbeds for northerns, we'd stop only to unhook fish or free snags. Doc didn't like trolling. He'd rather sit still and jig for walleyes. I told him that, being a dentist, he was used to standing in one place all day, jigging twenty-dollar bills out of patients' mouths. He couldn't quite accept the parallel between fishing and fillings, so we compromised. Troll in the morning, jig in the afternoon.

We hadn't paid much attention to topography

as we chewed the fat and our cigars, idling in and out of bays and between islands for the better part of the morning. At about noon, tummy time, we stopped for a nontraditional shore lunch of peanut butter sandwiches, salt and vinegar potato chips, a candy bar, and a cold thirst quencher.

We checked the map to see where we were, but we couldn't be sure. The lake was larger than lakes we'd fished in the past, and no landmarks screamed for attention. The aluminum boat bottom left a silver streak on the rock as we pushed off, preparing to jig for walleyes a few hours before heading back.

As we zigzagged from one productive walleye hole to the next, Doc talked about his kids, I talked about my lady friends, and we caught a lot of fish between the laughs and the lies. The sun began to sink above the tops of taller trees, when we decided to reel in and head for the cabin.

> *"Lost?" I said. The single word emerged as a long, quavering death sentence.*

We planned to aim north, staying close to shore until the cabin appeared on our left. After half an hour at full speed with the little Merc humming a happy tune, I cut the engine and got up to answer nature's call. Doc, holding a compass, was looking at the map trying to keep concern from his face.

"Looks like we have about one hour of daylight," I said in my best mountainman voice.

"We may need all of it," Doc said, not so encouragingly.

"Why's that?" I said, suspecting we were a bit off course, but not wanting to admit it.

"As far as I can tell, we're someplace north of Kansas City," Doc said. He wore a smile without much humor. He'd also let his cigar go out. This must really be serious.

"Lost?" I said. The single word emerged as a long, quavering death sentence to a routine outing in the Bush.

Doc said, "I think so," and I shivered, even though the temperature was 70 degrees.

I thought of when as a kid I had the run of miles of Iowa dirt roads and acres of corn and soybean fields. I explored forests of red elm, locust, willow, walnut, and oak. I scouted endless stretches of fence, ingrown with buckeye and butternut, broken only by wooden gates with baling wire hinges. But no matter where I'd traveled on my hikes and meanderings, I'd always found my way back home.

I've also been in some big cities, places where English isn't spoken much, like Atlanta and Chicago. I always found the way back to my hotel by using my memory, a street map, a cop, or a cab. But while fishing the lakes of Northwest Ontario, being lost takes on a whole new meaning. Sometimes maps and memories are useless, and you won't find a cop or a cab.

We decided on a desperation shortcut. We assessed the situation and determined we had plenty of boat gas. If we didn't make it back that night, we had bug spray to fight the skeeters, flashlights to scare the bears, matches to start a fire, and plenty of fish to eat.

Although it was still light enough to read the compass, the western shoreline was dimming fast. As we cut across what we figured was the main part of the lake, probably a couple miles wide, the water was smooth as glass. On the map, the lake tapered at the north end where the cabin stood, so we expected to see the dock at any moment.

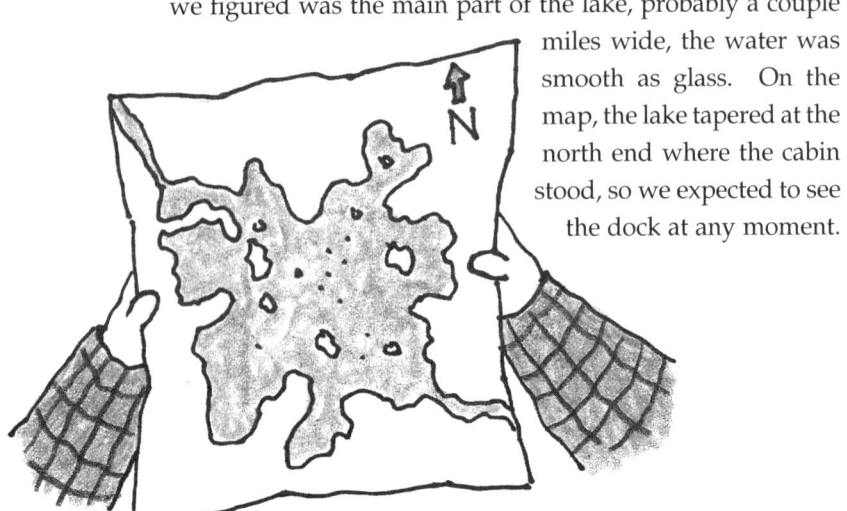

To our surprise and panic, the lake suddenly ended . . . in a weedbed? A dead end? We weren't in the main lake at all.

The questions we mumbled were all rhetorical: Did we pass by here today? Does that island look familiar? How much time do we have before dark? Are we out of cigars? You want to drive for a while? Are the rest of the guys out looking for us? Is your will up-to-date? Did you ever sleep with that redhead?

During the next half-hour of our frenzied flight, as our wake weaved northward from island to island, we found a few more dead ends. In the growing gloom, Doc said, "Let's turn left around this point." I figured this would send us to an untimely death as we plunged off the edge of the earth, but around the point I steered. There, in the sun's last light filtering through the birch and pines was . . . nothing remotely familiar.

The rocks became giant bilious leeches, praying for me to come closer.

I thought, this shouldn't happen to grown men, or me either. I slipped the engine into neutral and began to hallucinate. I jerked my hand back from the edge of the boat where the Swamp Thing was ready to drag me into a watery grave. On the nearby shore, trees turned into hideous arm-waving creatures hungering for human blood. The rocks became giant bilious leeches, praying for me to come closer.

On the verge of letting out a sobbing scream, I almost trashed my U-trousers when Doc yelled, "Look!" Blinking back the hysteria for an instant, I saw the aluminum skid-mark we'd left at lunch. An old friend. A beacon of heroic proportions. Back to civilization, as we knew it. Saved for sure. We'd trolled south to this point, so we could hug the western shore and find camp.

Two hours later, with flashlight batteries almost dead and our engine burning fumes, we tied up in front of the cabin. Through the windows, we could see the boys around the dinner table, raucous laughter mixed with the lapping of the lake. Doc and I unloaded the boat in silence, another adventure over, another day in the life.

The rest of the week we insisted to our buddies and to ourselves that we hadn't been lost at all; that we didn't think for a minute we'd be marooned indefinitely with the bears and the moose and the darkness. But we knew. We wouldn't forget.

I think often of that day with Doc. Although we both claim to have brought us back alive—he with his sharp eyes and me with my insistence on trolling—we agree that the next time we get lost, we'd just as soon do it together.

Thanks, Doc.

EPISODE 5

What To Do When The Fish Stop Biting And The Fishermen Start

Staggering amounts of time, money, and energy are invested by the average fisherman on the sport he loves. Some, like me and an ever varying group of five or six or seven others, go so far as to spend six days and nights in the Canadian Bush each year. Our primary purpose, in addition to the pursuit of unbridled sweet release from civilization, is to hook hordes of pike and walleyes.

For some reason, plumbing the depths of pristine lakes

appeals to us. Maybe it's the ambience of the remote wilderness of Northwest Ontario. Maybe it's the freedom from phones, the crush of people, and the turmoil of rush hour. Or maybe it's just being out with the guys and not worrying about orthodox speech and actions and the real or imagined limitations they impose on the masculine spirit. Whatever the reason, when we arrive at Sioux Lookout to board the de Havilland, we leave decorum and a good percentage of common sense behind.

> **We leave decorum and a good percentage of common sense behind.**

Some may call this annual outing a sophomoric relapse. Some may blame it on a return to primitive roots. And still others may label our six-day affliction temporary insanity. But whatever it is, our behavior is worth a closer look.

About Swearing—Sailors in the South Seas would be disgusted at our speech. It's as if we cross the border into a strange country where communication is possible only by replacing adjectives and many verbs with cusswords. Those of us who usually refrain from foul words must rely on a bilingual interpreter when speaking to rank members of the group.

About Gluttony—No moderation in the Bush. We punish ourselves mercilessly with food. Seems to be a contest. How much fried food can I eat? How many days in a row can I feast on onion-laced pork and beans? How many miniature Snickers candy bars can I inhale?

And even though most of us don't smoke, every man brings at least a week's supply of cheap cigars. At first, we light up to "keep the bugs away." But after the first day, we all 'gar up like it's our duty to maintain a burning throat and breath only an iguana could love.

About Gaseous Emissions—Onions. Fried fish. Sour cream potato chips. Garlic salt on scrambled eggs. Dry roasted peanuts. Peppermint schnapps. Kosher dill and Braunschweiger sandwiches. Enough to turn even the strongest stomach. And when it does, a double-barreled cacophony follows, so vile as to be life threatening within five yards of the perpetrator.

About Refuseitis—Of all the antisocial mannerisms adopted on these annual excursions, this one's the worst. A member of the party won't pull his weight. He decides he's on vacation so he won't chop wood, bail boats, or wash dishes.

Nobody knows exactly why, but at one point or another in the outing, each of us refuses to do his share, ignoring the friction it causes. And when the sparks fly, which usually coincides with a slowdown in fish bites, we're more concerned with fighting each other than with fighting the fish.

Refuseitis isn't an isolated incident applying only to our group. I've spoken to lots of fishermen who experienced the malady when they were isolated with three or more of their own kind. In fact, anyone who fishes or hunts with a group knows what can happen when refuseitis hits. And until a few years ago, I knew no cure.

Each year we choose a group chairman by voice vote. His duty is to contact the Canadian outfitter for a fly-in date and time, report on when the ice went out and how the fish are biting. He's also responsible for keeping the grocery list, for organizing a pretrip meeting to discuss the "must have" lures, and for exchanging greenbacks for Canadian currency to buy groceries.

When Doc was elected chairman, he handled his office well. He did exactly what was expected of him and then set new standards that removed the refuseitis syndrome forever.

Doc is my dentist. You'd think a doctor

would know better, but on our fly-in trips he enjoys his cigars and a massive intake of unhealthy food just like the rest of us. And although Doc doesn't act his age most of the time, he's a little older and, I would have to say, sometimes a little wiser than the rest of us.

At our pretrip meeting, we went through the motions of menu planning and the rest. When we thought the meeting was over and the time had come to break out the refreshments, Doc said, "Hold it!"

I thought, what's this? A chairman taking charge? We'd never seen anything like this. Momentarily stunned, we listened.

I thought, what's this? A chairman taking charge?

"I don't know about the rest of you guys, but I think everyone should be doing his fair share to make this trip a full six days of fun instead of three or four," he said.

"Awwww," we chorused. But we looked at each other and knew exactly what he was saying.

"To equal out the workload," he said, "and give everyone a little variety, here's what I propose." Doc handed each of us a sheet of paper with, can you believe it, individual job assignments.

"I've given this a lot of thought," he said, "and with some adjustments, I don't see why it won't work."

Eight of us went on the trip that year. And conveniently, eight job categories were listed: boats, wood, ice, water, fish guts, cabin cleaning, lanterns, and morale. Here's how each job broke down.

Boats—Each morning make sure boats are bailed and dry, tanks are topped off, and beverage containers are removed to garbage bags. Each evening make sure boats are tied to the dock.

Wood—Cut or gather enough wood for each day's needs, start and maintain fires for morning and evening warmth, and dump ashes when necessary.

Ice—Make sure coolers contain enough ice to cool refreshments for the next day. Keep refrigerator ice cube trays full.

Water—If the cabin doesn't have a pump (most don't), maintain a supply of relatively clean lake water for cooking and washing dishes. Also, fill plastic sun showers each morning so the water warms for evening.

Fish guts—Take fish remains far away from the cabin so gulls can feast.

Cabin cleaning—Sweep the floors, straighten up the cabin, and make sure garbage is bagged and out of the reach of woodland creatures, like 500-pound black bears.

Lanterns—Fill lanterns daily, replace mantles when necessary, pump 'em up, and keep 'em lit at night.

Morale—Keep the coffee pot perking, stock plenty of toilet paper and reading materials in the john, and track down and eliminate flies and mosquitoes in the cabin.

"Now, I've arbitrarily assigned each of us one of these jobs as our major responsibility for the entire week," Doc said.

"Is that all," somebody said. "Piece o' cake."

"Just one more thing," Doc said. "As you may notice, I left out the toughest and most unpopular chores. KP duty, fish cleaning, cooking, and, worst of all, dish washing." (Here came boos, hisses, and language usually reserved for the trip.) "But we'll handle that easily. I've split the group into four two-man teams who will rotate throughout the week."

Doc gave us a KP schedule. Amid groans and some laughs, Doc said gravely, "Come on guys. If you have a problem with this, get it out now. Because once we get to the Bush and the fish and the fun, there's gonna be no room for it." And not one of us could come up with a reason why it wouldn't work.

Since that year, with Doc at the helm, we've continued to break from civilization's mores by doing everything that brought us enjoyment before. We've carried our gluttony and gaseousness to unparalleled excess. But no outbreaks of refuseitis have appeared. Each man automatically discharges his menial task without pause or procrastination. And the burden associated with KP no longer exists.

This structured approach to vacation chores isn't overkill, but a workable solution suggested by a smart fisherman to solve a real problem.

Thanks, Doc.

EPISODE 6

Taking The Family Car On A Fishing Trip Is Driving A Hard Bargain

Sooner or later the time comes when a guy decides it's his turn to volunteer his car or truck or van for the annual stag fishing trip. I guess it has something to do with peer pressure or pulling one's own weight. Anyway, every year I joined an unlikely group of friends who took two or more vehicles to Canada. The gas cost was split among the six or eight of us who formed the fly-in fishing party. And it worked fine.

From previous years of riding with others, the first time I volunteered to drive I had a pretty good idea of the condition my family car would be in when it returned to Iowa from the drive to Sioux Lookout, Ontario. So when I arrived home safely after a week in the Bush with a cooler holding six beautiful walleye fillets, did my lovely lady welcome me with a smile and a big kiss? Hardly. As I swung open the car door, she took a whiff and said, "I've been in pool halls that smell better than that car! Don't come in until you clean it!"

I guess what her olfactory sense reacted to was a combination of body vapors from the 12-hour drive; the fumes from assorted food wrappers containing residues of onion rings, tacos, fries, and burgers; the reek of northern slime from my tennies; and the stench of the cheapest cigars money can buy.

As for the body odor, I'll admit I've been known to go without a bath for maybe a day or two. (Jumping into a Northwest Ontario lake so cold that soap won't lather is not my idea of necessary hygiene.) As far as the food wrappers go, hey, a guy has to eat, doesn't he? The only thing I know that will drown northern pew is an inch of grease in a frying pan. And the cigars? Well, boys will be fishermen. So will girls, I suppose.

After dumping the trash in the can and my gear in the garage, and hiding my favorite fishing tennies in the boat to age for later use, I hosed the car inside and out, scrubbed the coffee stains from the upholstery, and let it air for a few hours. I didn't get a meaningful welcome home smooch until after a shave, a shower, and a promise never to offer to drive our car to Canada again.

Comparing notes at the usual postfishing photo-swap meeting, I found that all of us who had volunteered our vehicles in years past had been met with the same homecoming and cleaning chore. I looked around the room and saw a few pigs in training, but by and large, we were a typical group of walleye fishermen out to have a good time and to live to lie about it.

Ten months passed before we had our first meeting to plan for our next week of walleye madness, coming up in June. One of the wives had managed to get pregnant and her due date was the same as our annual appointment with destiny. Another wife, without consulting the head of the household, had thoughtlessly phoned relatives in faraway places to announce plans to host a family reunion during that week. So it looked like only six of us would make the trek north. My dentist, a friend of mine I call "Doc," immediately volunteered to drive his car and take three of us. The attorney offered his van for the gear, so we were all set.

"Say, don't you drive a Cadillac, Doc?" asked the banker.

"Something wrong with that?" answered Doc.

"No, but we might trash it pretty bad." That brought chuckles from the rest of us.

I said, "Doc, why don't you take that boat anchor you call a station wagon? No way in the world could we hurt that piece o' junk."

"Nope," Doc said, lighting up one of his cheap cigars. "In the first place, the Caddy rides a lot better and is easier to drive. In the second place, that old wagon is okay for farm ponds, but I don't think she'd make it all the way to Sioux Lookout and back."

"What's your wife going to say when we turn that car into a landfill on wheels?"

Doc dragged on his cigar, blew out an incredible brown cloud of obviously carcinogenic particles and said, "She'll never know."

This revelation was met with a round of hoots, elbow jabs, and spilled refreshments from those of us who thought Doc's mind had turned to worms.

"Get serious, Doc! Your wife is going to have a cow, man!"

"You want me to drive or not?" Doc asked.

Hmmm. That brought us to thinking of the wrath we had felt from our own better halves, so we decided to let Doc face the unavoidable consequences. Better him than us. As we prepared to go home to sharpen our hooks and pack and repack our tackle boxes, the attorney was already warning us about spilling things on his van seats and threatening to make it a nonsmoking vehicle. Doc was suspiciously speechless.

Two months later, the vehicles loaded and gassed, we were on the road by early evening. We made Sioux Lookout without complications the next morning and flew out before noon. The weather was hot, but the fishing was spectacular. We even managed a daily bath and some suntanning. Meanwhile, in the parking lot at the fly-in outfitters, the ash tray full of cigar butts, the Big Mac wrappers, a couple of almost-empty milk cartons, and a few sticky Coke cans were festering, turning the interior of Doc's car into an unspeakable vile pit.

When the antique de Havilland float plane carried us back to civilization after a week of pure pleasure in the Bush and Doc unlocked the car door, the air that escaped was detected by the Distant Early Warning radar system a few miles away, nearly causing a Red Alert. I'm not saying mold spores that floated out were big, but some of them wore Levis and Reeboks.

With the four doors opened wide and a stiff breeze blowing through, we cut cards to see who would empty the offending refuse. The cop drew the deuce, but said he could hold his breath a long time, having had fire rescue training, so he wasn't in fear of his life. After an hour of loading the fish and gear and settling up with the outfitter, the Caddy interior was free of most offensive odors. But when Doc fired up the air conditioner, a cloud like the green fog in the Passover scene from "The Ten Commandments" movie poured from the vents. We bailed out and waited for the killer gas to dissipate into the surrounding countryside before setting out.

About 100 miles north of Des Moines after an all-night drive, Doc suggested by way of CB radio that we stop for breakfast at a place he knew. Road weary and two hours from a comfortable bed, we pulled off and trooped into a restaurant. All of us but Doc, that is. He disappeared down the street in what once passed for a Cadillac.

We ate our sausages, eggs, and waffles in silence, having just about used up our conversation during a week in the boats fishing and in the cabin during marathon card games. The coffee was good, the best we'd tasted in a while, so we savored a couple pots, while we reflected where Doc had gone. It took about an hour to eat and for the banker to figure out how much we each owed for food and fuel and who had won and lost money on the daily big-fish contests.

We headed for the door and there was Doc. "Where you been? We were about to leave without you."

"I've been out making my wife happy," Doc said, and pointed to the yellow Cadillac at the curb, possibly the cleanest car I'd ever seen. The paint shimmered, the chrome danced, the tires looked like they'd been spit polished. We gathered around this beauty as Doc opened the doors. The fragrance of fine Corinthian leather stroked my nostrils, and as I peered inside, I saw that every nook and cranny had been scrubbed and rubbed to a showroom gloss.

As we marveled at the transformation, Doc said. "After every one of these trips, no matter how careful we are, we make a mess of our vehicles. Then it's up to the owner to go home, catch hell from his wife, and completely worn out from a 12-hour drive, clean up the mess.

"We split the cost for the gas and the food," Doc continued. "So why not for cleaning our cars? We're all responsible for trashing them, so why not be responsible for the cleanup?"

"How much?" asked the banker, the fiscal conscience of the group.

"This was the $45 detail job," Doc said. "I made the appointment a week before we left to make sure I could get it done fast this morning. Two cars, we get a $10 discount."

"So you think we should stop here and clean the cars and split the tab every year?" I asked.

"Eighty bucks six ways?"

"That's all. I'm not talking about this year. My car needed a major cleanup, anyway. But it sure is going to save me a lot of headaches when I get home."

> We admired Doc's car, climbed in, and refrained from cheap cigars and spillage for the next two hours.

We admired Doc's car, climbed in, and refrained from cheap cigars and spillage for the next two hours. I spoke to Doc a few days later. He said his wife was just tickled that he had taken such good care of their car, and that she wouldn't mind if he volunteered to drive again.

After that year, we added Doc's suggestion into the budget. And the next time I volunteered to drive on our annual fishing trip, I returned with a shiny, fragrant family car, and better yet, a warm welcome from a lady happy to see us both.

Thanks, Doc.

EPISODE 7

Friends, Snorers, And Fishermen, Lend Me Your Ears

Doc's my best friend. At least I think he is, the way I define a best friend. We get along well when we're together, which isn't often these days. We like the same things, including redheaded women and fishing in Canada, not especially in that order. And we dislike the same things, including the Yankees and neckties, in that exact order.

Our differences of opinion have never resulted in fisticuffs, but they've been close enough to make us strangers for a week or two. Doc attributes our friendship to knowing when to talk and when to listen. It's just that simple.

I had some good friends when I was a kid. A one-room country schoolhouse with 28 kids in grades K through 9 didn't offer a lot of friendship options. So I had to make the best of the situation.

The dads of a couple students worked in stores or factories in nearby towns. The rest of the kids were from farm families. No rich kids and no poor kids, no ugly kids and no dumb kids. Just girls and boys of various ages thrown together for an education.

Several serious obstacles hindered friendship back then, the first being relative size. A bigger boy could probably whip you, and usually did. Boys the same size, you treated as equals. A smaller kid? You had the option of whipping him or protecting him. If he were your little brother, you could ignore him.

The second obstacle to friendship was jealousy. When the teacher picked a student to ring the morning bell for the week, former friends treated the bell ringer like a leper until his hitch was up or theirs began. Bell ringing was about as deep as jealousy went.

The other obstacle to childhood friendship was physical distance. The telephone was for bad news and business, not for jawing with buddies. So if you weren't within a 15-minute walk or bike ride, you weren't near enough to be close friends.

As I grew up, most of the childhood obstacles to friendship disappeared. But then, at a remote fly-in outpost with a bunch of seemingly incompatible guys, thrown together for fishing, I discovered the emotional obstacles to friendship.

For a good many years I've visited the wilds of Canada—Northwest Ontario to be exact—to fish for wily walleyes and nasty northern pike. I've been part of groups as large as a dozen and as small as four. And although the fishing has always been exceptional, the chemistry between the fishermen sometimes has not. But just as in a one-room schoolhouse, being unfriendly in a one-room cabin isn't an option, so you have to make the best of the situation.

I understand how different social, economic, and educational environments can affect behavior. But sometimes these behavioral aberrations are just flat unexpected.

Like the year six of us made the Canadian trip and the prominent attorney treated us to a week of the most amazing table manners I'd ever heard. Or when the banker threw a fit, as well as bottles and cans, and tore up several decks of cards when his luck turned sour.

And how about the dentist who emphatically swore he didn't snore, even when presented with tape recorded evidence of his chain saw massacre of our sleep. Or the plant manager who bummed toiletries, clothing, and tackle from the rest of us because he hadn't packed them.

The cop who went to bed early every night and set his alarm for 5:30 a.m. woke everyone else, but he didn't get up. And the writer who constantly emptied ashtrays, straightened the stacks of girlie magazines, and swept the cabin twice a day whether it needed to be swept or not.

Just little things. But in the course of six long days and nights, little things have a tendency to make even sane men forget the moon and howl at one another.

Doc (the snoring dentist) and I (the neatnik writer) had been on several of these trips. The first day of fishing together, we were appalled at the actions of our companions. So appalled, in fact, that I was ready to commit mayhem in the night. But Doc, his obnoxious snoring already mayhem enough, came up with a brilliant solution.

At breakfast the next day, as the cop slept through his alarm and the attorney slobbered down his scrambled eggs, Doc made an announcement.

"From now on, why don't we try different fishing partners every day? That way I'll get to spend an entire day in the

> **Being unfriendly in a one-room cabin isn't an option.**

boat with each of you jerks and find out if you're really as bad as you seem."

"How do we decide who gets whom?" I said, hanging up the dustpan and leaning the broom against the wall.

"Well, we could cut cards," Doc said, "but someone has torn up most of them (he gave the banker a look), and I'd hate to lose another deck so early in the week."

Doc took a scrap of paper from his pocket and said, "Here's the schedule." It looked workable.

"During my snoreless sleep last night," Doc said, "I figured five possible boat pairings for the five days we have left. After all that work, you doughheads better have fun."

A couple hoots and raspberries, and then, "If I'm going with you, Doc, I'll need to borrow some jigheads," the plant manager said.

"I'll go with anyone so long as he doesn't cheat me out of a trophy northern," the banker said.

So we woke the cop, lent the plant manager a few 1/8-ounce jigs, waited until the attorney wiped the remains of breakfast from his chin, and loaded the boats.

That week was the beginning of a new experience for me. All this time I'd thought the attorney's strong point was audible eating. But after a few hours of cranking in fish and swapping our life stories, he told me an oral abnormality made him eat so loudly, and he was talking to a specialist about getting it fixed. I also discovered that we shared the same problems raising a family.

It took me over an hour to get the cop up and moving when it was our turn to share a boat, but I learned he'd been putting in 20-hour days solving an especially tough case, and this trip was his literal salvation from the nuthouse.

The banker talked about an unhappy home, teenage kids, and a career that wasn't what he'd hoped for. I told him about my son and my divorce and my work; and we both sorted out a few things.

We've eliminated the emotional obstacles to our friendships by knowing when to talk and when to listen.

The plant manager was just as happy as he could possibly be. Everything in his life was right. As he borrowed a cheap cigar and a light from me, he made me promise not to tell the guys that he forgot things just to irritate us. He'd make it up in spades next year.

The last day as the boat pulled away from the cabin with Doc and me on board, we continued where we'd left off four days earlier. Close friends can do that. He said his wife had heard about a medication to stop his snoring. And I told the joke about the blue and red ribbons. He caught a five-pound walleye while I promised to try to be more of a slob if that would make the trip better for him.

The week ended with handshakes, "see-you-next-year," and the promise of lasting friendships. Because, even though we were different sizes, we had no bullies in the group and no jealousy to speak of, besides our admiration for Doc's new yellow rain suit and the banker's 16-pound northern. The physical distances that separate us between fishing trips often are bridged by phone or mail. And we've begun to eliminate the emotional obstacles to our friendships by knowing when to talk and when to listen. It's just that simple.

Thanks, Doc.

EPISODE 8

If You Let A Smile Be Your Umbrella, You'll Be One Miserable Fisherman

The drive from Des Moines to Sioux Lookout had been uneventful, although I occasionally had to awaken Doc to stop his snoring. The noise didn't bother me much, but Doc was behind the wheel at the time, and I feared for my life.

After crossing the border at International Falls, we made our usual stop at Dryden to buy groceries. Then we zipped on up to Sioux, where Knobby was waiting to greet us.

At least one man in our group or a member of our families had used Knobby Clark's fly-in service every year since 1968. He maintains outpost cabins on a string of lakes on the Cat River chain in Northwest Ontario. The fishing and excellent accommodations keep us coming back year after year.

"Welcome to Paradise," Knobby said, as he smiled broadly and shook hands all around. "Have a good trip, ay?"

Doc told Knobby how relaxing the drive had been. No wonder. He slept most of the way. Knobby's wife, Bobbie, helped us do some paperwork and made sure we all had fishing licenses.

"Will we be able to fly in this morning?" I asked.

"Soon as the Beaver brings another group out," Knobby said. "Might as well get your gear ready to load."

That's all we needed to hear. The banker and policeman backed their vehicles down to the water, and we began piling sleeping bags, boxes of food, and fishing tackle on the dock. The amount of gear we thought we needed to survive for a week in the Bush was amazing. But with Knobby's constant advice that we lighten our load, in the last 10 years, we'd probably reduced our total by 30 percent. Easier on Knobby's planes and easier on our backs, too.

About an hour later, the Beaver landed and taxied up to the dock. We helped the incoming party unload, taking special pains to get fishing reports. As usual, fishing was good, the bugs weren't too bad, and the weather had been short-sleeved exceptional.

Knobby gave the signal and we formed a line, passing our gear, heaviest first, up to the pilot who positioned it in the plane. A short 15 minutes later, we were in the air, fingers itching for the first fish.

Planes that fly into the Bush are some of the safest and most reliable in the sky. But they're awfully noisy. The attorney, a lousy skeet shooter but a good friend, brought each of us a set of ear plugs—for a fee, of course—which made the ride more comfortable.

After a scenic hour, we began our descent to the outpost we'd booked after last year's trip. As the Beaver banked on final approach, we strained to see the cabin we'd share for a week and the Lund boats tied neatly alongside the dock. The excitement was as intense as the first time I'd flown in, 20 years ago.

One more hour and the chores of unloading and setting up camp were completed. We rigged rods and picked boat partners. Paired with Doc the first day, I fired up the new Evinrude while he tied on a jig. The sky was robin's egg blue, and the early afternoon sun offered the promise of a warm wonderful week.

That night, the walleye fillets were delicious. The six of us slept like proverbial rocks, at least until about four in the morning when the rain marched on the roof like an army of jackhammers.

I pulled the sleeping bag up around my chin and remembered what Knobby told us many years ago. "In this part of Canada, this time of year, you have three-day rains, and you have five-day rains. It usually won't rain hard in the daytime, ay, just a steady drizzle that keeps planes out of the air. But, worse than that, rain makes unprepared fishermen unhappy."

Listening to the rain splashing on the roof, I thought back, to a lifetime and 30 pounds ago, when I was a rank amateur to this brand of wilderness fishing. I was sure I'd taken all the necessary precautions when the rain began to fall. As we bailed the boats, the low clouds looked foreboding. It wasn't raining too hard, so I had every reason to believe the day would be wonderful.

"Ready to go?" Doc asked. Doc is my dentist, so I was

somewhat shocked to see him out of uniform, looking like Big Bird in his bright yellow rain suit. When he walked, the heavy suit made him sound as if he were covered with feathers.

"I guess so, Doc," I said. "The boat is about as dry as it's going to get."

I put my tackle box in the boat and was reaching for my rod when I noticed Doc staring at me. "Problem?" I asked.

"What's that you have on?"

"The best two-piece rain gear that five bucks can buy," I said proudly. "You like it?" I turned and modeled the see-through unit for him. He didn't look impressed.

"You think it will keep you dry?" Doc asked.

"Of course it will," I said, sitting down to give the engine starter rope a yank. "It's guaran . . ." and the pants ripped from the waist in the back to the snaps at the crotch ". . . teed," I finished.

"A guarantee won't do much good out here, will it?"

I examined the parting of my plastic pants. "Now, how did that happen?" I asked, with a grain of disbelief.

"Could have been poor workmanship, poor materials, any number of things," Doc said. "And what's on your feet?"

"Boat shoes."

"Well," Doc said reflectively, "when the bottom of the boat begins to fill with rain water, they'll be submarine sneakers."

"Oh, I'll be all right," I said. "The temperature has to be at least 65 degrees, and it won't rain much."

In answer to my meteorological naiveté, the sky opened and began raining cats, dogs, aardvarks, and assorted reptiles. We sought refuge in the cabin until the worst had passed.

As I took off my damaged rain duds, intent on somehow patching them, Doc lit one of the unbelievably foul cigars from his regretfully inexhaustible supply and said, "I don't understand."

"What's that, Doc?"

"When it comes to your rods and reels and line, you go first class. But then you buy your rain gear at a Ma and Pa Kettle garage sale."

> **The sky opened and began raining cats, dogs, aardvarks, and assorted reptiles.**

"That's because tackle is for fishing," I said, as I tried a safety pin to hold the crotch together, then thought better of it and took it out. "A rain suit doesn't have much to do with fishing."

"Ah-ha!" Doc exclaimed. "That's where you're wrong. How do you expect to concentrate on your presentation when your shorts have more water in them than is in the lake?"

"Maybe it won't rain that much," I said hopefully, as steady rain obscured the lake from view.

"Yeah," Doc said. "And maybe bears in the woods use toilet paper."

I was finishing up my patch job using a hotel sewing kit to stitch electrical tape to the crotch seam. As I surveyed my handiwork, Doc said, "Want some advice?"

"I have a feeling I'm gonna get it, whether I want it or not."

"The pleasure quotient of the total fishing experience is directly proportional to the comfort of the fisherman," Doc said.

"What does that mean in plain English?" I asked.

"Next year, get yourself a good rain suit," Doc said.

We fished in the rain all that day and the next two. I recall it was a three-dayer, as Knobby had forecast. The outstanding fishing almost, but not quite, took my mind off my waterlogged butt. And when the sun shone brightly for the rest of our stay, the fishing was just as good, but I enjoyed it even more.

My thoughts abruptly returned from the past as the policeman raised a racket making coffee and starting a fire to ward off the morning chill.

One by one, we hit the deck and dressed. After breakfast, we checked knots and tackle and prepared for another fishing day.

"You gonna catch Mr. Big today?" Doc asked, peering out at the rain-splashed lake.

"Several Mr. Bigs," I said, zipping up my tailored rain suit. "Want to hand me those boots?"

Doc picked up the warm, waterproof Sorels, admired them for a second, then handed them over with a smile and said, "Nice." And I said,

"Thanks, Doc."

EPISODE 9

With The Outboard In Gear, The Brain Must Not Be In Neutral

I was at the helm of the 14-foot Lund, my hand lightly on the tiller. The pristine wake bubbled from the mirror-smooth water and rolled shoreward. With a million and six scattered islands, I had to continually check the map to get my bearings. In the meantime, I dreamily enjoyed the drone of the little Evinrude.

As usual, we'd driven to Sioux Lookout and flown into the Bush in one of Knobby Clark's float planes for a week of outstanding camaraderie and fishing.

Splashing along on either side of me were the boats containing the rest of my group. We'd made the Canadian trip for the umpteenth year in a row. On my left were the attorney and the banker; on the right were the policeman and the plant manager. All three engines ran wide open, humming in synch as we motored across the mile-wide main lake in search of yet another walleye honey hole.

As the TV commercial says, "Boys, it doesn't get any better than this."

My mind was a fog of semiconsciousness as I breathed the intoxicating combination of fresh Ontario air and motor fumes, interrupted occasionally by clouds of smoke billowing from one of Doc's six-for-a-dollar cigars. The morning sun was warm as Doc, my dentist, relaxed in the bow, opening an icy cold refreshment. As the TV commercial says, "Boys, it doesn't get any better than this."

Then, BAM! I was in the bottom of the boat along with assorted jigs, spoons, and Lazy Ikes. Doc was standing on his head up front, Diet Coke saturating the elbows of his L.L. Bean chamois shirt.

Righting myself, I climbed back onto the seat and hit the kill switch to stop the howling engine. Doc had bitten through his 'gar and was beating the glowing embers from his life vest. Though the anchor rope was wrapped around his throat, all in one breath he uttered an amazingly colorful string of phrases that questioned my parentage and suggested impractical things to do with his boots and my body parts.

As I set my tackle box upright, the hooks and lures scattered, following those that had already fallen.

"You all right, Doc?"

Doc answered in a short unintelligible burst as he freed himself from the braided polyester noose. When we stood up, the boat didn't move. It was like standing on dry land.

"We've either been attacked by the Loch Ness monster's Canadian cousin," Doc said, "or someone put a rock in the middle of the lake."

I peered cautiously over the side to assess the situation. Sure enough, we were sitting atop a big flat rock that looked a lot like the roof of a 1963 Coupe de Ville. It was maybe a quarter of an inch under the surface, just as wide as the boat and 10 feet long.

I checked the motor and was relieved to find the skeg had lost some paint, but was otherwise unharmed.

"Two million square miles of 30-foot-deep lake and you find the only rock," the attorney jeered.

"I've heard of walking on water," the policeman snorted, "but this is ridiculous!"

"Do you come here often?" the banker laughed as he beat the side of his boat.

"Now you know how the captain of the Titanic must have felt," the plant manager added. "Abandon ship! Walleyes and children first!"

The initial mockery over, we now had to figure out how to free the boat. After we cleaned up the scattered tackle, Doc lit another stinkweed. I picked up an oar to knock it out of his mouth, but thinking better of it, I tried to push us off instead. But not enough rock was visible.

The policeman tossed us a rope and tried to pull us off. No good. The keel must have been wedged in a crack. Then both boats pulled. That didn't work, either.

I suggested we leave the shipwreck as a marker for other unfortunate seafarers. But Doc said, "Let's lighten the load."

As I was about to throw his new graphite rig overboard, Doc protested profanely. He eventually calmed down enough to direct the other boats to pull alongside.

We climbed aboard, and with a combination of engine power and manpower, we managed to jerk free. A closer look at the rock revealed ancient aluminum scrapes, of other poor souls who had met the same fate.

Merrily on our way again, Doc burned a hole in my map with the business end of his 'gar to mark the approximate spot of the rock.

"Next time, steer clear of the black hole," Doc said, poking his pinky through the charred circle. I guessed I was forgiven, because of the weird smile on his face. Anyway we discovered an outstanding mother lode of walleyes, so the day became a phenomenal success. Just before dusk, we avoided the stony beast on our way back to the cabin by taking the safer southern route.

That evening, after a feast of fresh fish, Doc put a hypothetical question to us: "What would you have done if you were alone in that boat when it ran aground?"

"I'd swim ashore and get help," the attorney said.

"Too far," Doc said. "And remember, it's late May. Even if you were wearing a life vest, hypothermia would get you in 200 yards, let alone half a mile."

"Then I'd dump the gas and use the tank as a float to keep my upper body out of the water. I think I could kick like crazy and make it . . . if the water were calm like today. Otherwise, guess I'd sit tight and wait for someone to miss me. I'd run the engine to stay warm at night, and I'd eat walleye sushi until help arrived."

The policeman, giving the matter deep analysis, scratched the stubble of his four-day beard and said, "I think I'd stay put until I saw a plane; then I'd wave my shirt to get their attention. If that didn't work, I'd soak my T-shirt in boat gas, stuff it in an empty tackle box, and when I heard a plane, I'd float it on the water and set it on fire. The oil-mix gas and burning plastic would give off plenty of black smoke before burning through. Maybe I'd add chartreuse twister tails for good measure. Up here in the north woods, pilots are alert for smoke."

"Not a bad idea," Doc said. "But what if you didn't have a match or a lighter? What then?"

"I'd fly a kite," the plant manager said.

"That sounds fun," the attorney snickered.

"No, really. I'd break down my ultralight rod for the frame, fold my lake map into a diamond, and stitch it together with four-pound test. Then I'd attach it to my heavy-duty trolling rig and go kite fishing. A pilot passing within a few miles couldn't miss something as strange as a kite flying 150 feet up from the middle of the Bush," the plant manager explained.

"Kite fishing. I like that," Doc said. "And if there weren't enough wind?"

"If my life were in danger from a lightning storm, I'd use the gas tank idea and swim for shore."

"How about you?" Doc asked the banker.

The banker, ultraconservative in everything but playing cutthroat pitch, said, "I'd stay with the boat. After all, it's out in the middle of the lake, so any other boats or passing planes would have a good chance of seeing me. Other members in my party would eventually come looking for me. And while I waited, I'd try some lures I've never caught fish on."

"That should keep you busy for several weeks," I said, to a lusty round of chortles and guffaws.

"You got a better idea, Mr. Navigator?" the banker asked.

"Touché, mon ami," I said in my best Italian or whatever language it was. "As Doc suggested today, I'd lighten the load. I'd tie all the gear I could on a rope and hang it over the side, using my boat cushion and life vest for a float. Then I'd hop out and try to move the bow around until I could stand on the rock and use it for leverage. If the boat was still too heavy, I'd break the oar in two and maybe work the round pieces under the keel to roll it off. If that didn't work, I'd empty most of the gas tank, take the engine off, tie it to the floating tank, and float it alongside while I worked with the oar. And if that didn't do it..."

"Whoa!" Doc said. "You guys really are getting into this."

"Isn't that the idea?" the banker asked.

"Sure is," Doc answered. "We get up here in the middle of nowhere and vegetate. Some people (he gave me an evil stare) even go to sleep while driving a boat. Although the environment is relatively friendly this time of year, it can be a killer if not treated with alert respect. I thought this exercise would make us think 'What if?' and get our creative juices flowing. And it worked."

> *Doc looked thoughtfully around the cabin and replied, "I'd use my cellular phone to call AAA."*

Although we haven't exactly immersed ourselves in brain busters on every one of our subsequent fishing trips, with Doc's help, we have occasionally explored new cerebral territory. In the process, we've discovered the interesting personalities of our fishing buddies and the native resourcefulness of our own minds.

"We haven't heard from you yet, Doc," the attorney said. "How would you get the boat off the rock?"

After several puffs on his cigar and through a blue-gray haze that smelled like a cross between sour milk and the inside of a goat, Doc looked thoughtfully around the cabin and replied, "I'd use my cellular phone to call AAA."

Why didn't I think of that?

Thanks, Doc.

EPISODE 10

A Sharp Hook Meeting A Dull Mind Can Be A Bloody Shame

I have a healthy respect for the pointy end of a fishhook. That's probably because, in my reckless youth, I managed to impale myself with some regularity. I thought those days were long gone until I joined the guys for another trip into the Canadian wilderness.

As tradition dictated, six of us gathered in Iowa on a warm evening the first Friday in June. We became part of the caravan of fishermen headed north for the border crossing at International Falls. The hundreds of cars and campers and pickups barely outnumbered the deer that stood next to the highway between Cloquet and Virginia.

Our overnight trek to Sioux Lookout, Ontario, was made more memorable by a speeding ticket in Minneapolis and a stop to photograph two moose outside Dryden. I told Doc, my lead-footed dentist, that I'd send him copies of my moose photos. He told me he'd make sure I got a copy of his cancelled check to the Minnesota Department of Public Safety. Doc was so mad that he almost chewed through his cigar. Fine with me. Anything to stop the stench.

When we pulled into Sioux Lookout, Knobby Clark had the de Havilland Beaver gassed up and ready to go. As in the past, we'd reserved one of Knobby's outpost cabins on a large lake about an hour's fly-in due north. After some paperwork and loading our food and gear, Knobby's daughter Kim lifted the plane smoothly off the water. We were once again on the way to a "walleye wonderland."

The first days of fishing were all we'd hoped for and more. The 'eyes were in a feeding frenzy. As a bonus, the northerns we hooked were all five pounds and over; no snakes in the bunch. This was a light-tackle paradise.

But all good things come to an end. A cold front brought a day of drizzle and the most dismal angling we'd ever seen.

Doc and I returned to spots where we'd caught fish the previous three days, but managed to fool only a few loners. The rain let up, but the wind made boat control impossible.

I dragged a jig and crawler through a likely spot and caught a magnificent bedrock specimen while Doc wrestled with the motor and hooked a stump. Doc broke off his snag and I finessed my jig loose just before we ran aground on a rocky point. Following a broken oar and socially unacceptable remarks that echoed through the sodden pines, we again made our way to open water.

Doc tried his hand at backtrolling into the whitecaps; it took only four or five minutes to bail out the boat. Then he somehow coaxed a good northern to the boat. It was deeply hooked, so Doc brought it on board for minor surgery. It spit the hook, tail-kicked my new needle nosed pliers into 16 feet of water, and did a few laps around the bottom of the boat. After surrounding the critter, returning him to the lake, and washing off layers of slime, our hands resembled prunes with fingernails.

We stopped in a protected cove for shore lunch, but the mosquitoes were lunching there, too. So we wolfed down a few soggy bites between swattings and headed back to the choppy, but relatively bug-free water across the narrows. Ending up pressed against a sheer rock wall by the wind, we almost gave up for the day. Anyone observing us from long-range would have assumed we were having a wonderful time.

"You want to go back to the cabin and get beat at cribbage or stay here and get beat by the waves?" I asked Doc, as he sat hunkered down in his dripping rain gear.

"I think I'll try some heavy-duty tackle and go after Mr. Big," Doc replied. He was always a hard man to reason with if he had any chance to catch a fish. Then, as if to justify his madness: "Experts say bad weather is the best time to catch hogs."

"Swine experts or fish experts?" I asked.

Doc rummaged around in his tackle box and pulled out a Professor #3 two-tone silver and copper spoon with a treble hook you could have stuck three grapefruit on. Then he grabbed the new baitcasting outfit he'd practiced backlashes with the day before. He fastened the spoon on a ball-bearing swivel attached to a mile of 20-pound-test line and an 18-inch chromium steel leader. Doc was so proud of the rig, he decided to light up a 'gar before beating the water to a froth in search of his trophy.

The aroma of mildewed turnips spread through the pristine Canadian mist. If I hadn't been upwind, I'd have been asphyxiated. As I turned my head for more breathable air, Doc made a two-fisted power cast. Pow!

My face went numb, and Doc was saying something that sounded like, "Oh, my."

Why couldn't I see? Was it raining harder? Doc was repeating my name in a strange voice. What was happening?

Then, somewhere from that remote part of my brain where fear and panic reside, came the realization that Doc's lure had hit me.

"Is it my eye? My eye? Is it my eye?" I asked Doc, somewhat surprised I could speak in the dark.

"Nooo," he moaned.

I was sure it was my eye. "My eye? Doc, is it my eye?" I couldn't see anything; then not much; then the buzzing in my head began to wear off. I blinked and closed one eye and then the other. There was light. When I finally could see out of both eyes, I saw the look on Doc's face. "What is it?" I asked, for some reason out of breath.

> **"Is it my eye? My eye? Is it my eye?" I asked.**

"I don't know," Doc answered.

Ten, maybe 15 seconds had passed. I tried to figure out why Doc couldn't tell me where I was injured. Then I looked down and wondered who had butchered the 4-H Grand Champion Hereford on the front of my new yellow raincoat.

"Where did it get me, Doc?"

"I don't know," he repeated. (Later, I accused him of leaving his pre-med training back at some Iowa City fraternity house.) He reached into his tackle box and pulled out an old sweat sock. Not sanitary operating room protocol, but with nothing else dry within reach, I took it and began mopping my face.

On the second mop, I touched my nose and located the point of impact. I also became aware that Doc's sock hadn't been washed since high school gym class 20 years ago.

After a few splashes of water and gentle wipes of the sock, I discovered that my nose, just below the tip and above the philtrum—I looked it up when I got home—had suffered a combination of blunt and not-so-blunt trauma. One of the hooks had ripped right through.

While I cautiously surveyed the damage, Doc began a string of apologies. I tried to listen to the more grovelling ones—free lifetime dental care and reimbursement for my plastic surgery bills—but I was more concerned with surveying the cut.

"Doc, will ya give me that spoon?" I asked, pointing at the

attempted murder weapon.

"What for? You going to check it for fingerprints?" As he handed it over, I saw the line end in a great blue heron's nest on his reel.

"No, I just want to use it for a mirror," I said. The curvature made my reflection look like someone from a fun house, but I could see that my snagged sniffer wouldn't probably require stitches.

"You all right?" Doc asked.

"I think so," I said, wincing at the throbbing pain that replaced the numbness. "But I'll check with my attorney to make sure." (Fortunately, my attorney was also on the trip.) "How did this happen, Doc?" I asked, pulling the blood-soaked sock away long enough to point at my rosy nose.

"Well," Doc said, "when I cast, I think the spoon hit the rock wall on the backstroke, ricocheted, and wrapped around your head. With this rain suit hood on, I didn't think there'd be a clearance problem." He paused. "To tell the truth, I wasn't thinking about clearance at all. I just cast without checking." Another pause. "Good thing you were wearing glasses."

I took off my glasses and squeegeed the raindrops with prune fingers. In dead center of the right lens was a big ding where the edge of the Professor #3 had made contact. Hitting the wall must have slowed the speed enough to only scratch my plastic lens instead of breaking it.

"Are your glasses scratched?" Doc asked.

"Correction," I said. "Are my very expensive glasses scratched? Yes, they are."

"Well, my homeowner's insurance will cover them. Just send me the bill."

"Does your insurance cover permanent disfigurement?" I asked.

"I think so," Doc said.

"Pain and suffering?"

"It should."

"Cribbage losses?"

"Come on," Doc said. "I really feel terrible about this. Can't you see I'm sorry? Give me a break."

I'd never had Doc over a barrel like this. It seemed he always had the upper hand in everything. So I'd make him suffer a little longer. What if the tables were turned? Would he make me suffer through my guilt? You bet he would!

So I said, "I'll think about it, Doc. You know, I see it not as an accident; it was a careless mistake. You of all people should have known better. I'll probably have a jagged little scar to look at in the bathroom mirror every morning for the rest of my life. What reminder will you have? We've been friends for a long time, Doc, so I think you can understand that for right now, sorry's not enough."

"I think I know how you feel," Doc said dejectedly, "but I'm not exactly enjoying my stupidity, either."

"You have no idea how good it is to hear you're not perfect, Doc," I said. "You want to keep fishing for Mr. Big or call it a day?"

"Let's go back, get the first aid kit, and rinse the cut with peroxide," Doc said. "I don't want you to get athlete's nose from that sock."

When I laughed, the bleeding started again.

Doc and I stopped talking about my nose injury a long time ago. I let his insurance company buy me a new pair of glasses. And a steak dinner took care of the pain and suffering. The scar only shows up when I get a tan, which isn't often.

But let's back up. On the way to the cabin that day, Doc asked, "By the way, when was your last tetanus shot?"

"Oh, about 15 years ago," I said. "You think I need one?"

"Probably not," Doc said, taking another puff on his horsehair cigar. "I try to keep my hooks clean."

Before my jaws locked up, I said,

"Thanks, Doc."

EPISODE 11

Every Now And Then, A Fisherman Needs A Tune-up

Night sounds in the Northwest Ontario Bush are foreign to civilized ears from farther south. No jet planes, police sirens, or blaring radios. Instead, the throbbing of a ruffed grouse, the melancholy laugh of a loon, and the rustle of leaves and pines riding high on the breeze. The voice of nature speaks in the satisfied stillness as it has for countless centuries.

The six of us who made the annual walleye quest (a dentist, an attorney, a banker, a policeman, a plant manager, and I) valued the sounds of silence so much we outlawed radios and tape players. So when we drove to Sioux Lookout and began loading one of Knobby Clark's float planes for the ride into the Bush, I was as surprised as Knobby was to see a strange addition to our fishing gear.

"What's this?" Knobby asked, opening the black hourglass case. "You going to serenade the walleyes or fish for 'em?"

Doc, my friend when he wasn't shooting me full of Novocain, said, "That's a guitar, Knobby."

"I guessed that," Knobby replied. "Fishing rods don't have six strings and a sound hole. It's just that, in 20 years, I can't remember anyone taking a guitar." Knobby ran a finger across the strings and listened to them vibrate. "Do you play, Doc?" he asked.

"Nope," Doc said. Then, throwing a thumb in my direction, he said, "But he does."

I'd been known to bend a string or two, but for years I'd resisted Doc's suggestions to drag along one of my guitars. I didn't want the hassle. In spite of my annual protest, Doc borrowed this one from his son.

"Doc," I said, "between catching bushels of walleyes and kicking your tail at cribbage, I don't think I'll have time to tickle the strings."

"If there's room on the plane, it's going," Doc said, snapping the case closed and looking hopefully at Knobby, then at the Beaver already crammed with gear.

"At least it doesn't weigh much," Knobby said, as he handed the guitar to the pilot who secured it with a rope to the top of the food boxes. Then he said, "Get on board, men! The walleyes are waiting!"

The first three days we were up at dawn, fishing like maniacs until darkness obscured our rod tips. We collectively caught and released hundreds of walleyes between 2 and 4 pounds. And the few for the dinner table were the best we'd ever eaten. The fishing experience we'd longed for all year had come to us like a wildcatter's gusher coming in. But as we finished a leisurely breakfast on the fourth day, shuffled down to the dock, topped off the gas tanks, and took our sweet time motoring out to the honey holes, it was apparent that our excitement level had slipped a few notches.

"I need a vacation," Doc said, as he stretched out on the boat seat, his head propped up on a seat cushion, his boots dangling over the side of the 14-foot Lund. He was taking a break after mechanically jig-hooking two dozen of the most beautiful walleyes ever to come out of a Canadian lake. A green cigar smoldered between his clenched teeth, every putrid puff reeking like an August road-killed skunk.

"What do you call this if not a vacation?" I asked absentmindedly, as I returned my 20th fish of the morning to the black water and maneuvered the boat to send Doc's rotten smoke downwind.

"It's relaxing, all right," Doc said. "But when fishing is this good, it doesn't take long for relaxation to become boredom."

I stifled a yawn and dumped overboard a cup of more grounds than coffee. (I never have been much good at stove-top percolators.) "Yeah, I know what you mean," I said, lowering a jig with a chartreuse twister tail. "There comes a time when you think, Hey! What's the point?"

"Let's try a new spot," Doc said. "Maybe the fish will be harder to catch somewhere else so we'll have more fun."

"I'm having fun now," I said, setting the hook into another 3-pounder. "Maybe we just need a new challenge."

Doc peering out from under the rim of his Iowa Hawkeye ball cap, said, "I hope you're not thinking what I think you're thinking." With every syllable, small mustard-colored clouds that smelled of burning cow horns rose from the end of his cigar.

I freed the walleye and said, "For a change of pace, let's take a ride on the wild side!" I throttled the little Evinrude up to cruising speed.

For a change of pace, let's take a ride on the wild side!

Although Doc hated to troll for northerns, I talked him into rigging his baitcaster with a big spoon; we tried some rock walls and fished alongside reedbeds. By the time we'd each pulled in a dozen pike—some hatchet handles and some nearing 6 pounds—the sun disappeared in a black cloud. As Doc washed the fish slime from his hands, he said, "I think I've had about all I can stand."

As the first drop of rain extinguished Doc's cigar, we hightailed it to the cabin. Although we had plenty of rain gear along, the prospect of heading back out that miserable afternoon to catch another boatload of easy fish wasn't appealing. We tied up the boat and made the 50-yard dash to the cabin just as rain began pelting down in earnest.

After hanging up our life vests, I helped the policeman fill and pump up the Coleman lanterns while Doc made fresh coffee. The attorney got the fire fixin's ready to compensate for dropping temperatures. We chowed down on a lunch of bologna and peanut butter sandwiches laced with sweet pickles. The plant manager and the banker brought out some illustrated reading material, and Doc beat me in two out of three noisy games of cribbage. I retired from the competition to let someone else try Doc's luck and crawled into bed for a short nap. I dropped off, listening to rain massaging the cabin roof.

When I awoke refreshed an hour or so later, the rain had subsided, but low clouds blocked any hint of sunlight. The cups and crumbs and potato chip bags on the table had been replaced by an assortment of pots arranged in a semicircle, with a plastic dish pan upended in the middle. Two aluminum lids were suspended from the rafters, and the policeman was pouring uncooked rice into two empty pork and bean cans. "What's going on here?" I asked.

"Trying to make some maracas," the policeman said, as he sealed one of the cans with duct tape and gave it a shake. I rubbed my eyes to make sure I was really awake. Over by the fire, the attorney was carefully wrapping a comb in wax paper. The banker had strung a leather shoestring through a hole in the bottom of a plastic bucket and tied the other end to a broomstick. Adjusting the tension as he plucked the string, he seemed pleased with the results. The plant manager was blowing across the tops of several bottles filled to varying levels. He sipped from one or another to adjust the tone.

"Did I miss something while

TUNE-UP 65

I was asleep, Doc?" I asked.

"Not at all," he said, handing me the guitar. "You're just in time." I took the guitar and noticed a Fender medium pick, my favorite, wedged under the strings. "Just in time for the first Kezik Lake concert," Doc said, obviously pleased with himself.

"Oh, yeah?" I said. "What instrument do you play?"

"Don't have to," Doc said. "I'm the promoter." (A good thing because Doc has about as much rhythm as a three-toed sloth.) Lighting up one of his stinkweeds, which gave off the aroma of radishes cooked in formaldehyde, and sinking into an overstuffed chair, he said, "Gentlemen, it's showtime!"

> We played and sang and hooted and hollered every Buddy Holly, Elvis, and Everly Brothers tune we could remember.

With that, the policeman pulled two drumsticks from his back pocket and began beating the dishpan, pots, and pan-lid cymbals. The banker-bassman followed the rhythm with a run on his shoestring, and the attorney hummed along on his comb.

I cranked a couple guitar strings up to pitch and strummed a few tentative chords. Next thing I knew, we were in "Rock 'n' Roll Heaven." We played and sang and hooted and hollered every Buddy Holly, Elvis, and Everly Brothers tune we could remember. Then we ran through my personal favorites by the Beatles, followed by the Turtles, Stone Poneys, Eagles, and all the animal groups in between.

When we forgot the words, the attorney with his comb or the policeman with his makeshift Ludwigs filled in the gaps. The plant manager tried all afternoon to get the fluid levels right in his bottles, but overcompensated with the blackberry schnapps and ended up clapping his hands and grinning instead of playing.

When the drummer tired of the sticks, he shook his pork-and-bean maracas to "Michael Row the Boat Ashore," "Where Have All the Flowers Gone?" and Doc's old favorite,

"Greenfields."

Our concert lasted maybe three hours and ended as abruptly as it had begun. The comb was unwrapped, the shoestring bass unstrung, and the pots returned to the shelves by the stove. I wiped my sweat from the guitar neck and put the old girl tenderly in her case.

As I stepped outside for a welcome breath of odorless air, I noticed that the Bush creatures had gained control. The loons and gulls were chatting and the mosquitoes had resumed their buzzing search. Doc joined me on the deck, sans cigar, and we wordlessly watched a mother grouse and her four baby grousettes stroll by. "Paradise Regained."

I don't know when I ever felt better. Our music ringing through the pristine Bush had amplified my senses and renewed my enthusiasm for fishing. I listened as the boats rhythmically caressed the dock. I watched cotton candy clouds lift and melt away. And when the sky filled with stars that night, I could feel their sharp cold light through my flannel shirt.

Doc uttered a satisfied, "Ahhhhh."

"Was that the break you needed?" I asked.

"Just what the doctor ordered," he said. "I'm ready to be a fisherman again."

I knew exactly what he meant.

The next three days were filled with the purest pleasure anyone can get from a rod, a reel, a boat, and a lake filled with fish. Maybe we didn't work at it as hard as before, but we relished each catch and appreciated each fish.

When the Beaver skimmed in to return us to Sioux, leaving was more painful than ever.

Some say the best of times can't be repeated. But, I'll always hold my memory of that magic time in the wilderness when I got high with a little help from my friends.

Thanks, Doc.

EPISODE 12

Few Wives Who Refuse To Bait A Hook Willingly Sanction A Stag Fishing Trip

About a lifetime and a half ago when I was young and single, taking off on a week-long walleye fishing trip was a no-brainer. I put new line on my reels, crammed my tackle box with jigs, gassed up the Ford Fairlane, picked up the guys, and headed north. But when I became matrimonially involved, additional guidance became necessary.

A definite strategy is involved in obtaining permission from a spouse or significant other to spend joint income on something other than food, shelter, and anniversary gifts.

For some reason, few wives who refuse to bait a hook willingly sanction the expense of a stag fishing trip for their till death do us partners. But bless their little hearts, they think nothing of blowing the same amount of cash on custom country goose curtains for the kitchen. Doesn't make sense.

Way back when the Mr. Coffee we got as a wedding gift still worked, my scheduled June 1st fly-in trip to the Canadian Bush was coming up in little over a month. I had just gotten off the phone with Knobby Clark who owned the fly-in service in Sioux Lookout, Ontario. Knobby said the ice was not quite out, and because of heavy snow, the water would probably be higher than normal when we arrived.

A new cabin had been built on the outpost lake we chose, and the boats had new outboards, as usual. Knobby was looking forward to seeing the six of us for the tenth year in a row.

When we hung up, I was itching to call the rest of the guys with the news. My finger had almost made it to the telephone dial when snookums called me to dinner. Dutifully, I sat down to eat.

"Who was that?" she asked.

"Knobby Clark from Sioux Lookout. You remember my talking about him, don't you?"

"No." The lie ricocheted around the room like a Star Wars laser beam. Could be trouble. I quickly changed the subject.

"Ohhhh, Smoochmistress," I said. "Mmm-mm. This really looks yummy. You sure are a good cook, Babycakes," I added with some effort. She looked at me strangely, but it was enough to throw her off track for a second or two while I gathered my thoughts.

I had just smothered the entree with Tabasco when my wife said, "Why don't you spend your vacation at home this year? We can use the money for something that really matters, like kitchen cabinets."

I failed to see any meaningful comparison between coaxing a hog walleye from the bottom of the lake on four-pound test and putting our old dishes in new cabinets. But I wisely chose not to make that observation.

Then she said, "I have a great idea. Let's invite my mother to stay for a week. How about the first week in June?" (Choke!) "We'll take her to Ottumwa and Cedar Rapids to visit my aunts." (Gag!)

To keep from putting my 9D in my mouth, I clenched my jaw. Hard. I needed serious help to overcome her anti-fishing attitude.

To keep from putting my 9D in my mouth, I clenched my jaw. Hard. I needed serious help to overcome her anti-fishing attitude.

"That would be a lot more fun than going on some old fishing trip with Doc and the rest of the boys. Don't you think?"

When I didn't answer, she must have thought I agreed.

"Good! Then it's settled. I'll call Mom tonight."

"Youch!" My fork clattered to the table, and I held my hand over my mouth in a show of acute discomfort.

"What's the matter, Honey?" she asked.

"I think I chipped a tooth on something in the, uh, meat loaf, Dear. Better go see Doc right away!" Before she had time to see through the bluff, I was out the door, in the car, and headed over the river and through the woods to Doc's house. Doc, my best fishing buddy, conveniently is also my dentist, so I hoped my sudden flight from home wouldn't raise too much suspicion.

When I arrived at Doc's 20 minutes later, I punched the doorbell and his wife appeared. "Hi, is Doc home?" I asked, my face smeared with desperation and a little Tabasco.

"Come on in. He's out on the back porch with one of those things he smokes" (Mrs. Doc wrinkled her nose). Unaware that cigars should contain at least some part of the tobacco plant, Doc ordered his by the metric ton from some third-world country.

In my opinion, Mrs. Doc was in a separate category as far

as wives go. I was in her debt for saving my bacon on several occasions when visits to Doc's game room with the rest of the guys got out of hand.

Once she called my wife, saying the ballgame had gone into double overtime and I'd be home soon. That gave us a chance to play two more games of cutthroat pitch. If Doc hadn't mooned on a queen-six, I'd have broken even.

Another time, Mrs. Doc called my wife to tell her I was helping the Adel Volunteer Fire Department put out a grass fire and not to wait up. It was 4 a.m. before we got the poker chips put away, but there was Mrs. Doc rubbing Doc's cigar ashes on my cheek, to give me an authentic fire-fighter look. After eight hours sitting next to Doc's smudge pot, I already had the authentic smell. Yes, Mrs. Doc is one in a million. Maybe two.

Out on the screened porch, Doc sat puffing on one of the vilest tarpaper and dandelion root stogies I'd ever come across. The night was warm. As a fan blew most of the smoke toward the big oak trees in the backyard, I expected to see squirrels fall from the upper branches, overcome by the toxic cloud. I pulled up a chair behind the fan.

"Doc, there's trouble in River City," I said. "I don't think my new bride will let me go to Canada this year." If I didn't have a tear in my eye, I should have.

"Can I help?" Doc asked.

"You're probably the only one who can," I moaned.

He looked me over like a coach sending in a rookie to snatch victory from the jaws of certain defeat. "Are you willing to take a few chances?"

"So I can go fishing in Paradise? You betcha."

"If you do it right, you'll have no need for outright lies or other foolishness that could jeopardize your happy home," Doc said. "Are you willing to follow my instructions?"

"Anything you say, Doc."

He asked Mrs. Doc to bring a pencil and pad of paper, then invited her to sit in on the discussion. She declined, voicing possible female conflicts of interest. Besides, she had papers to correct for one of the classes she taught. Doc gave her a peck on the cheek and she went back inside.

> *If you do it right, you'll have no need for outright lies or other foolishness that could jeopardize your happy home.*

"The first thing," Doc said, "is the timetable. We have exactly 36 days and a wake-up before we head for Sioux Lookout." He numbered lines on the paper from 36 to one. It took two sheets.

"From now on," he said, "each day you'll have to do specific things to get into your little lady's good graces. If you do it right, she'll not only give you permission to go this year, but she may also make it standard operating procedure in years to come."

Doc completed the list in about an hour. Here's a sample:

Day-35—Take her out for a seafood dinner. Observe that the red snapper or mahi-mahi is good, but not nearly so delicious as the walleyes you've caught and brought back from the Canadian Bush for 10 straight years.

Day-32—Tell your cuddle bunny not to worry about cleaning the house this weekend. The housekeeper you hired starts Monday.

Day-26—Insist that your little darling relax and watch TV while you do the dishes and fold the laundry. And even though the Royals and the Yankees game is on, sit through "Love Boat" and "Fantasy Island" reruns, all the while rubbing her tired feet.

Day-21—Beg her highness to call in sick so you can give

her the attention she so richly deserves for an entire day, beginning with breakfast in bed. If that works (doubtful) don't burn the toast. If it doesn't work, show enough affection to slow her down, but not enough to make her late for work.

Day-18—Convince her that you're excited about her mother coming to stay for a week, but how about when the weather is nicer, say July? And a week is hardly long enough, is it? Ask Mom to spend a month. She can even have your bed. You'll sleep on the couch.

Day-14—Bring home a stack of travel brochures with exotic Caribbean destinations. Tell the bathing beauty you married what a thrill it will be to whisk her away next winter to an island paradise. Stuff a $20 bill in the cookie jar as proof you're serious about saving for the trip.

Day-10—Stock the freezer with ice cream treats and the pantry with cookies and chocolates. Tell your skinny minnie to go ahead and eat anything she wants, because a few extra pounds just means more of her to love.

Day-7—Send flowers to her at work for no apparent reason with a card that reads, "Every day we're together brings an eternity of happiness. Thank you, my love, for being my wife." The other ladies in the office will envy her for being married to such a wonderful, romantic guy. She'll feel special.

Day-4—Gather obituaries with pictures of men your age from as many newspapers as you can. Spread them out on the kitchen table and let her find you sadly reading them. Tell her that life is sooo short, and you could go just like that. (Snap your fingers.)

Tell her you'd like just one more kiss from her sweet lips, just one more fishing trip with the boys before the Grim Reaper strikes. And then tell her she'll be well provided for when you're gone, because you'll have your life insurance doubled the minute you return from Canada.

Day-2—Secretly invite that co-worker of yours and his wife to stop by after dinner with their new baby. Act surprised when they arrive. Hold the baby as much as possible and offer to change its diapers, even when they really need changing.

After they leave, steer your mommy-to-be into the spare room where you have all your fishing tackle stacked and your bags packed for the trip. Tell her the room would make a great nursery, and maybe it's time to seriously consider beginning that family she's always wanted.

"Day-two is the perfect time," Doc said. "Don't wait any longer to ask for permission to go on the trip. If all goes well, her only logical answer will be, 'Yes, my love.' "

Doc leaned back, satisfied with his handiwork, the black eye of his expired cigar clenched in his teeth, the sure-fire strategy in place.

I took the list gratefully. As I was getting up to leave, Doc said, "So you broke a tooth eating meat loaf?"

"How? Don't tell me she called before I got here?"

"Yup," Doc said. "And she wants to see X-rays."

"You're kidding! You're not! What am I going to do?"

Doc reached into his shirt pocket and handed me a small manila envelope. "Here's a chipped-tooth X-ray. A molar. Second from the back on the left. Just so happens you have a crown there already. She'll never know."

Doc's checklist worked. By Day-21, my wife volunteered her permission. I didn't even have to ask. Of course, she held me to many of the promises I'd made, like the Caribbean vacation and the doubled life insurance. And our son will be 12 next month. But what a small price to pay for a fishing trip with the guys.

The only real sacrifice I made was when my mother-in-law visited for the entire month of July. When she wasn't sleeping in my bed, she was instructing me from the back seat as I chauffeured her around the state.

What goes around comes around, however. When Mother developed a bad toothache, I suggested she go see Doc. Good dentist and good friend that he is, he accepted her as a patient immediately and performed two root canals in just one day.

Thanks, Doc.

EPISODE 13

Walleyes Aren't Always Greener On The Other Side Of The Rapids

"I think we need some excitement," Doc said.

"Howzat?" I asked. I was tying on another eighth-ounce jig after breaking off on a snag, and I was giving my dentist-fisherman friend about an eighth ounce of my attention.

"Let's go shoot some white water," Doc said.

That gave me such a scare I almost stuck the hook through

my thumb. We were on one of many lakes on the Cat River chain in Northwest Ontario. Most of the time the chain is a basic bunch of lakes connected by small rock-strewn streams. But this time of year, early June, those streams are raging, boiling torrents of snowmelt, punctuated now and then by rocks that look like the tailfins on a 1957 Chevy, only sharper.

Now that Doc had my attention, he said, "Think of the pool below the rapids. Think of the huge walleyes lying there, waiting for fishermen who have the guts to go after them."

"No, Doc," I said.

"Awww, come on," he pleaded. "It'll be fun. I'll even let you run the engine."

"Not a chance, Doc," I said.

"Well, why not?" he asked impatiently.

"Those rank cigars of yours must have brought on some sort of amnesia," I said. "If you can't recall what happened the last time we shot some white water, you need major psychiatric help."

Six or eight years earlier, our regular group—the policeman, the attorney, the plant manager, the banker, and Doc and I—arrived at Sioux Lookout. Knobby Clark gave us the go-ahead to load the de Havilland Beaver with our food and fishing gear, but he couldn't fly us into the Bush until the morning fog lifted. That year we had chosen his Wesleyan Lake outpost. With time to kill, we gathered around Knobby's office counter and watched as he marked prime walleye spots on the lake map.

"Drift through this narrows," he said, jabbing the map with a ballpoint pen, "and you'll catch a limit of walleyes in 10 minutes." Grinning widely, we all stared at the ink spot, itching to be there.

But Doc, always one to stumble to the tune of a different drummer, asked, "What's down here, Knobby?"

Knobby looked where Doc was pointing his finger, almost off the edge of the map, and said, "Danger."

"What's so dangerous about it?" Doc asked.

"That's where Wesleyan empties into Bamaji," Knobby explained. "This soon after ice-out, the water is fast. Lots of rocks. A waterfall at the bottom. Portage around the rapids if you want to take a look, but be careful."

"Anybody ever hurt there?" Doc asked, a look of prurient interest in the macabre glowing in his eyes.

"They say a boatload of foolish fishermen overturned a long time ago," Knobby said. "They say a couple men drowned. I don't know for sure if the story is true, but when you see those rapids and rocks, you'll believe it happened."

Immediately discounting the danger factor, Doc asked, "Is the fishing any good below the rapids?"

"The fishing is good on all my lakes," Knobby answered, trying to head Doc's suicidal thoughts off at the pass. "If you want to fish on the Bamaji side, use the portage to get downstream. The portage bypasses the rapids that cut sharp to the right, run into a deep pool, then go over the falls. It's about a 75-yard portage down to the pool, but I suggest you leave your boats up above. Here." Knobby pointed to a spot on the map above the rapids. For good measure, he left Doc with a final warning. "If you get too close to the white water, the current will suck your boat right in, and I won't be responsible for . . . the consequences."

Knobby looked where Doc was pointing his finger, almost off the edge of the map, and said, "Danger."

We shuddered at what those consequences might be. All of us but Doc, that is, who was in the process of removing the cellophane wrapper from a large cigar. The attorney observed it looked a lot like something a St. Bernard would leave on its kennel floor. When Doc lit up, the odor indicated that the attorney's powers of observation were on target. Doc took the cigar outside following our unanimous threat to throw him out. Through the window, I thought I saw gulls drop below the fog to get a look at what had died, but none came closer to Doc than absolutely necessary.

When the sky cleared before noon, we were airborne in minutes, headed due north on a beautiful Canadian day. A little over an hour later, the pilot buzzed the rapids to give us an aerial view of our potential watery grave. I don't think Doc was impressed.

The plane set down on the main lake, the pontoons ripping the glassy surface as we approached the outpost camp. Three Lunds with brand new engines were tied on one side of the dock. The A-frame cabin that would be our home for the next six days wore a fresh coat of red paint. Our decision to use Knobby's fly-in service was once again justified.

During the first few days, we fished the upper part of the lake, gradually working our way south along sheer rock walls and back into quiet coves lined with reeds and beaver-gnawed timber. Out on the lake was pure paradise, but near shore, gnats, black flies, and mosquitoes had never been so bad. Whichever bug dope we tried was like putting whipped cream on a piece of pumpkin pie; it made us tastier.

At shore lunch one day, Doc, my boat partner, yelled, "Let's go shoot some white water!" He was sitting by himself on a big rock about 30 feet away. We had requested that he move out of nose range when he put fire to another of his cigars, so he had to talk pretty loud for us to hear him.

"You're crazy!" the policeman yelled back. "We're catching all the good walleyes we can stand."

And the banker added, "Yeah, Doc, why should we chance the rapids?"

Doc took an Olympic-size puff on his 'gar just as the wind changed, and we scattered as the raw umber cloud floated toward us. As it cut a deadly swath through the swarms of insects, they rained in suffocated heaps on the lichen-covered rocks. Even after the cloud dissipated, the air retained the flavor of a sewer backup at a sauerkraut factory.

"Let's at least go scout the area," Doc said. "If it looks too dangerous, we don't have to try it."

Although out of character for Daredevil Doc, his cautious comment made sense to me, so I agreed to join him.

Leaving the other four men to fish safer spots, Doc and I motored south past picturesque islands bristling with pines, into a narrow flume. We caught a few small northerns and one or two walleyes along the way, but holding the boat became tricky in the quickening current.

I took the lookout position at the bow and called out steering instructions. Doc tilted the little outboard to miss rocks that littered the bottom like 2-7-10 splits at a bowling alley. We were probably 100 yards from the rapids, but we could hear the rush of water, and the current was getting faster every foot. Over to the right, as Knobby had explained, was the portage. Doc cut the engine and we beached the boat.

A clearing about a boat and a half wide had been chopped through the small trees and brush. A neat row of logs lay across the clearing from one end of the portage to the other, to serve as rollers for taking a boat through. We grabbed some light tackle and made our way to the pool on the other side. With each step we kicked up a gazillion mosquitoes that we batted at, but couldn't outrun.

At the end of the portage, the rapids emptied into a large pool of deep black water, still, except for a few swirls—a nasty current at work. On the far side, the pool dropped off maybe three or four vertical feet over a distance of 20 or 30 feet into the lake beyond. The water looked like a huge mound of Jell-O as it rushed over the top. It wasn't Niagara, but we figured it was the waterfall Knobby had told us about.

Due to overhanging limbs and slippery rocks, access to the pool from shore was restricted to a casting area of no more than six feet, so we had to take turns. Doc was the first to toss a jig and twister. It barely broke the surface when a 3-pound walleye took it and ran. As Doc was releasing the gorgeous dark-green creature, I hooked its twin, and before I could land it, Doc crowded in with another just like it.

"Can you imagine the size the walleyes must be in the far side of the pool?" Doc asked.

Now just as excited as Doc, I said, "And can you imagine the monsters below the falls?"

"It's so close, but so far," Doc replied sadly. Then he brightened and said, "We could drag our boat over here through the portage, but I don't know if we could make it over the falls."

> *The water looked like a huge mound of Jell-O as it rushed over the top.*

"Or if we could get back," I said. We caught a few more fat fish on a few more casts and were trying to figure out how to go about getting where the Godzilla Walleyes lived, when the sound of an outboard pierced the air. It wasn't any 7 1/2-horsepower unit, that was for sure, and the sound was getting louder.

Suddenly, a boat carrying four Indians jumped the waterfall. We could see "15" on the Evinrude engine cover. The boat made a couple zigzags and disappeared toward the white water. Instinctively, we cringed, set our teeth, and waited for the sound of propeller on rock, but it never came, and the engine hum disappeared as the boat headed north into Wesleyan. (Knobby told us later that the Indians from a nearby Ojibway village were probably checking traps and maintaining a weather station in the area.)

"What do you think?" Doc asked.

"I don't know," I said. "They have a lot bigger engine."

"And we have a lot smaller boat," Doc said.

"But they know what they're doing," I said, hoping Doc would come to his senses.

"Let's give it a try," Doc said. "I don't think we'll have any problem." And he was off like a shot, running through the portage like a senator on his way to a pork barrel.

By the time I caught up with him, he was using the anchor

rope to tie tackle boxes, gas tank, and the rest of the gear to the boat seats. "If we're not going to have a problem," I asked suspiciously, "why are you lashing everything to the boat?"

"In case we capsize, we won't lose anything," Doc said. At the time it sounded reasonable, so I helped secure the last of the rods and gave my life vest zipper an extra tug to make sure the Royal Canadian Mounted Police would at least be able to recover my bruised and water-logged remains.

With Doc at the tiller, I pushed us out and we began our run downstream to the land of jumbo walleyes. We'd gone maybe six feet when we hit the first rock. That killed the engine. Doc tried to yank the starter rope, but in the five seconds it took him to remember that the engine wouldn't start while in gear, we'd been pulled sideways into the current and were sliding toward the rabid jaws of the rapids. From there a series of bone-crunching collisions bounced us from rock to rock. Doc had given up on the engine by that time and had pulled it out of the water. It was then he uttered the wisest words spoken all day: "Hang on!"

Most disasters happen fast. No time to think of anything except self-preservation and, in my case, a fleeting thought of that magnificent redhead from St. Paul. We were both in the bottom of the boat, keeping company with northern slime, bent hooks, and worm parts. In less than 20 seconds, we breathed a sigh of relief, peeked over the gunnel, and saw we had arrived in the pool.

"Man, that was . . . " Doc said, as we began to climb back onto our seats. And the boat took a gut-wrenching, roller coaster plunge down the face of the falls.

After bailing water, we spent the next hour trying to motor back up the slick waterfall into the pool, but the engine was too small. So Doc dropped me on shore and I fought through the tangled underbrush and colonies of sparrow-size mosquitoes to finally arrive at the downstream portage point. Doc managed to climb the falls after several runs, motored through the pool, and was nursing the stub of a smoldering cigar while he waited for me.

"That was kind of fun," Doc said.

I'd have strangled him where he sat, but the stogie stench kept me at bay. "So, are you going to try the rapids now, hot shot?" I asked. "Or was it so much fun you want to stay here all night?"

Before he could answer, the Indians zoomed by on their way back to Bamaji, not even touching a rock or varying engine speed. Amazing. So Doc tried to find a path through the rocky rapids for about 20 minutes while I swatted at mosquitoes. He killed the engine several times and was washed over the falls twice, but managed to buzz right back again with no trouble. On one attempt, he made his way about halfway up the rapids. The engine was at full throttle, but the boat made no headway, so Doc backed off and came over to my resting spot. The ground around me was littered with hundreds of crushed skeeters, and my face, ears, neck, and hands were smeared with blood and insect parts.

"We have two possibilities," Doc said. "First is to portage the boat, motor, and everything in it. It will be dark in about an hour, and we might be able to finish by then, if we hurry. The second possibility is to lighten the boat so the engine can push it up the rapids. What do you want to do?"

I was too sweaty and tired and chewed up to care, so I simply said, "Let's lighten the boat." I realized that meant I'd be carrying two anchors, two tackle boxes, a depthfinder, a small cooler, and the rest of the gear. It would take several trips, but we had no better option for getting back to our home lake and back to the cabin.

Doc helped me unload the boat and was about to shove off when he paused and said, "Here, have a cigar. They keep the bugs away."

With that, Doc handed me one of his green gaggers and offered a light. I was reluctant at first, but desperate. I soon found that I could hold my breath while puffing, and I set to work. I took the tackle boxes on my first trip and was surprised when Doc pulled the boat into shore at the upstream portage as I arrived. Less weight had done it.

"Only three more loads," I said, and turned to get them.

"Let me go," Doc said. "I need the exercise."

While I put the tackle boxes in the boat and continued to puff away, Doc trudged on out of sight. It had been a long hard day, and I looked forward to cleaning up and having a relaxing evening before the next day's fishing frenzy. Now that our white-water adventure was safely over, I even looked forward to contriving lies about it.

Doc returned with the depthfinder and net, then the rods and cooler. I watched as he made his last trip. With an anchor in each hand, he couldn't slap at the swarms of thirsty critters that bit and drank from every inch of his exposed skin. Only after he put his load into the boat was he able to mash a few dozen for some relief.

"Let's get out on the water," Doc said, flailing the air around his head. "These bugs are outrageous."

"Why don't you light up a cigar?" I asked, flipping what was left of mine into the water. "They smell bad, but they sure work good."

"No time," Doc said. "Let's just get going."

We were almost back to the cabin 30 minutes later before I realized why Doc hadn't lit up an insect-repelling cigar when he went after the gear. He had given me his last one.

The tale we told the guys that night about our Northwest Ontario Passage has since been embellished. To this day, however, whenever Doc suggests we shoot some white water, I tell him I don't need another dose of excitement quite like that one.

As I recall, it took a tube of toothpaste and a loaf of garlic bread to erase the taste of that revolting cigar from my mouth. But I'll never forget the unselfish friend who helped turn a foul afternoon into a sweet memory.

Thanks, Doc.

EPISODE 14

Bush Hog Buffet

Barring bad weather, the float plane would splash down early the next morning, returning us to Sioux Lookout after our annual week of walleye fishing and fraternizing in the Northwest Ontario Bush.

We'd already eaten our final walleye supper, washed and stowed the dishes, and were in the process of cleaning the outpost cabin for the next fishing party. Doc, holding an unopened plastic jug of chunky pink liquid, had a strange look on his face.

"What's that?" I asked.

"Looks to me like a gallon of Thousand Island dressing,"

Doc said. "Lucky for us we bought two gallons of the stuff. We might have run out."

Then he picked up what appeared to be three giant elephant tusks wrapped in plastic and waved them in the air.

"And here are 600 incredibly cheap styrofoam cups," Doc announced. "I thought we'd be drinking coffee out of northern skulls by Wednesday, but somehow our cup supply lasted all week."

Our fellow anglers stopped sweeping and packing gear to observe the biting edge of Doc's wit as it cut through the clouds of cabin dust.

"Whoa! Look at this!" Doc dropped the cups, grabbed seven family-size boxes of Ohio kitchen matches, and stacked them high on the table. I noticed it was potentially a towering Blue Tip inferno.

"We might have had to rub sticks together!" Doc cried. "Good thing we were prepared!"

Doc threw open the refrigerator door. "Nooo!" he screamed in mock anguish. "Only three dozen eggs! How will the six of us make it through breakfast in the morning?"

Doc is my full-time friend and sometime dentist. In the years I'd known him, I'd never seen him act so crazy, especially sober. As he rummaged through the antique gas refrigerator, he continued, "Three heads of lettuce, a pound of cheese, two packages of cold cuts, and a pound and a half of butter."

"Okay, Doc," I said. "What's your point?"

He slowly closed the refrigerator, glared upward disgustedly at the four loaves of bread, five pounds of onions and ten pounds of potatoes on top of it, and sat down at the table. Intrigued, the boys gathered 'round, leaning on brooms and telescoping rod cases.

"See these matches?" Doc said.

A one-eyed duck could have seen that many matches

from 500 feet during a rain storm.

"Each of these boxes contains 250 matches," Doc explained. "Seven boxes, uh..."

"Seventeen-fifty," offered the banker.

"Thanks. That's 1,750 matches. During our six days in the Bush, we need to light the stove burners maybe three times a day. But the stove has a pilot light. We need to light the gas lanterns when it gets dark. But they have automatic ignitions. We need to light our cigars..."

> **Then the fog rolled in on little cats' feet.**

To add emphasis, Doc withdrew a swamp-green stogie from his fishing vest pocket, removed the wrapper and began to reach for a box of matches.

"But wait!" he yelled. "What's this?" And he pulled a Bic lighter out of his pants pocket. "How many of us have lighters in our pockets right now?"

Sheepishly, we each produced a lighter. The policeman, who didn't smoke, had two.

"And we each have at least one in our tackle boxes, don't we?" Doc asked, already knowing the answer. "So why did we buy matches for this trip?"

"Because we do it every year?" I volunteered.

"Exactly," Doc replied. "There's no way in the world we'd ever use that many matches. The same goes for the cups, and the eggs, and the dressing. We are prisoners of past routines, doomed to the same surplus inventory, year after year."

At the time, Doc was a relative newcomer to the group. So the attorney, the group's senior veteran and self-proclaimed Sage of the Bush, decided to educate Doc as to the excess.

"About eight or nine years ago," the attorney began, in his best Perry Mason voice, "12 guys made the trip. Good weather for six days gave us big appetites." He rubbed his ample paunch. "Then the fog rolled in on little cats' feet." (He walked his fingers across the table, showing off his limited knowledge of Carl Sandburg, as well as the gash from that afternoon's terrorist pike attack.) "And the plane couldn't fly in to get us, so our stay was extended by two and a half days."

Doc listened patiently as he puffed on a 'gar that smelled like a cross between rotted potato peelings and a summertime two-holer.

"We had eaten fish at least once a day all week," the attorney continued. "But while we waited for the plane, we had nothing to eat but fish, and fish, and more fish. No bread or peanut butter or bologna or cookies or anything else. Since we were out of syrup, we even used all the remaining pancake batter to make the ever popular fish-in-a-blanket entree. By the time the plane returned us to civilization, half of us were growing Y-bones, and the rest were looking for a sand bottom to spawn on. After recovering, we all decided never to run short of food again.

"So, Doc, we always start with a 12-man menu and prorate for how many make the trip. If we have six or fewer men, like this year, we cut it in half, then add provisions for one more man for the week. For seven or more, we cut it in half, then add provisions for two. I'll agree we got carried away with the cups and matches, but the rest is pretty close if we're marooned here another day or two."

A smattering of applause broke out at the eloquent summation.

"I rest my case, your honor," the attorney said.

Doc thought it over, then asked, "How old were you nine years ago?"

The attorney said something about the question being irrelevant and immaterial, and the banker said, "He was 28."

"Don't you think," Doc said, "that your eating habits have changed considerably in nine years? Less cholesterol, smaller portions, maybe a little healthier food? I mean, when I joined the group, the only way we knew how to prepare fish was to soak it in egg batter and fry it in about a quart of grease. Now we bake and broil and poach and even barbecue them."

"I get it," the policeman said. "You think we should haul in less food and get by cheaper without going hungry."

"It's not the money I'm talking about," Doc said. "Food is the cheapest part of the trip. No, it's the waste that bothers me. Our last night here and we have enough perishable provisions left to open an outfitting business. For some reason, from year to year we never seem to remember what we had enough of and what we ran short of. And not only food. I see individual overkill on other things, too. How many first aid kits?" Doc called for a show of hands.

Four first aid kits between six men.

"How many cans of bug spray?"

Three had two, two had one, and the plant manager had three.

"How about screwdrivers and other tools?"

All of us had the basic pliers and screwdriver in our tackle boxes. The policeman also packed a ballpeen hammer, a hacksaw, and enough wrenches to pull the transmission from a '56 Buick.

"With the pressure we get every year to lighten our fly-in load," Doc said, "I think we should make a standardized list of food and non-food items and stick to it. That way, we won't have to bring in stuff we'll never use."

Since that sounded like a reasonable idea, and since the fumes from Doc's cigar were about to gag us, everyone agreed. Then we evacuated the cabin to get some fresh night air while Doc put pencil to paper.

On the way out, the plant manager and I snatched our ultralight rigs, a handful of jigs and plastic tails, and headed for the lake. It was one of those late spring Canadian nights usually reserved for dreams. Air touched us like a chamois glove, warm enough to be comfortable in jeans and a flannel shirt, but cool and breezy enough to keep the skeeters grounded. The sky hung hazy, with a smudge of moon. We could just about see to tie knots and distinguish where we were standing on the rocks above the lake's gurgling black-marble floor.

Fifty paces behind the cabin, a pool of water slowly swirled, 20 yards from a small rapids. We cast 1/8-ounce jigs to the edge of the fast water, then tenderly worked them over the boulders through the pool, as the other three guys watched.

> Walleye after wonderful walleye splashed and kicked on 4-pound test. Neither fisherman nor audience spoke.

Walleye after wonderful walleye splashed and kicked on 4-pound test, then were released, unharmed. Neither fisherman nor audience spoke. No need. No contest for biggest, best, or most. It was our last and most meaningful moment of the week, a fleeting experience we had grown to crave, yet seldom experienced enough.

After what seemed like eight hours, but probably was closer to one, we reeled in and hooked our jigs to our rod eyelets. With our batteries recharged for another year, we shuffled back to the cabin.

"How's it going, Doc?" I asked as I broke down my rod and reel.

Doc saw the look in my eyes and knew I'd just had my final fishing fix. He'd get his in the morning. He liked to wait until the last minute because he felt it lasted longer that way.

"It's going good," Doc said. "Being an average guy with an average appetite, I figured out what I ate this week, to the closest potato chip. What do you think of this?"

I noticed that Doc's 'gar had died an unnatural death in the top of a Coke can, so I felt safe sitting down. The list contained everything from bacon and cheese to bologna and onions, detailing pounds or fractions of pounds of each consumed.

As I finished reading, Doc said, "All we have to do is multiply by the number of men in the fishing party, and we shouldn't have to worry about leftovers or coming up short if we spend an extra day. Of course, we'll revise it after we all review it, but I think it's pretty close. You probably noticed that everything on the list is perishable or better fresh."

"I'll admit that year-old hamburger can taste a little gamy," I said, "but where are the matches and the salt and pepper?"

"The salt and pepper and extra butane lighters, not matches, are in the chop box," Doc said. "Just as on an African safari, we'll have a special box of necessities that remains the same, no matter the size of the party.

"The person in charge makes sure the contents are replenished before each trip. That includes lantern mantles, aspirin, Band-Aids in a first aid kit, dish soap, garbage bags, aluminum foil, special cooking utensils like spatulas, a tool kit, playing cards, paper and a couple pens, bug dope, and lots more. The chop box is community property. So as with transportation and food, we'll split the cost among the members of the group. That means less to buy, less to pack, and less to waste."

The policeman caught the end of the explanation and asked, "How about the pork and beans, Doc?"

"We seem to buy just right for most of the canned goods," Doc said, "so those quantities won't change much."

"And how about the styro cups?" the attorney asked. "Where do they fit in?"

"They don't," Doc said. "I think we can get along just fine with a nice set of thermal cups and glasses that can be washed instead of tossed. They'll go in the chop box, too, and we can put our names on them. Less trash to fly out and less chance to turn this place into a remote landfill."

"This is too simple," the banker said. "Where's your spirit of conspicuous consumption?"

"I guess I lost it when I gained a renewed respect for myself and for the Canadian Bush," Doc said. "While I don't think it can get any better than this, it sure can get worse. And we're the only ones who can stop that from happening."

> **While I don't think it can get any better than this, it sure can get worse.**

I thought about Doc's comments that night. His words were still on my mind as I heard him slip out early the next morning to feel the final magical tug of a walleye on his line.

The chop box idea works fine, although some of us have had quite a struggle fighting the urge to be over-prepared and over-fed. But with just a little prompting and more careful provision planning, we've become more conscious of preserving our aging selves, as well as the fishing experience we love.

Thanks, Doc.

EPISODE 15

Brain Backlash

A flip of the wrist whizzed line off the baitcast reel, sending a sinking Rapala toward a stump submerged in 8 feet of Canadian lake. I pulled up sharply on my rod tip and thumbed the spool, dropping the lure in front of the stump, exactly where I wanted it. BAM! The walleye hit on the first wiggle, just as I thought it would. I set the hook and prepared to reel in the beauty.

But the crank wouldn't turn. The 150 yards of 8-pound test once wound tightly and evenly across and around the spool now looked like swamp moss hanging from a South Carolina cypress.

I snatched a handful of the tangle, hoping to back it off and free the spool for the retrieve. The heavy walleye made a freedom pull. Snap! Gone! Along with my lure and most of my patience.

"That's why I don't use a baitcaster," Doc said, calmly removing the yellowed cellophane wrapper from another of his inexhaustible supply of rotten cigars.

"I don't care about your tackle preference right now, Doc," I said disgustedly, sitting down in the little Lund and tugging line that refused to cooperate.

With his Bic set on blowtorch, Doc lit the cigar and blew a thunderhead of smoke into the Northwest Ontario air. The atrocious stench suggested a length of wombat intestine stuffed with shredded snow tires from a Studebaker Lark. "No matter what kind of anti-backlash magnetic, leather or boron composite braking system," Doc said, "with a baitcaster, you'll have problems."

I had freed about two feet of line and was ready to attack the snarl with a fillet knife. "Doc," I whined, "how can the line be a mess all the way through the reel?" I always ask Doc these kinds of questions because he always has answers—for the most part convincing, some possibly based on fact. But I wasn't prepared for what followed.

"It's simple," he began. "The spool of a multiplier reel, like your baitcaster, winds line in multiple coils, like a rizzle bender. When you cast, the spool actually spins at a higher speed nearest the axle bindle than where the main line plays out at the flam. When you thumb the tray and stop its movement, the rill spins inside for a microsecond. So the backlash begins framis from the inside vortex and travels out." He took another puff on his 'gar, quite pleased with himself.

I had been listening as closely as I could, getting nowhere on the bird's nest, but I suspected something odd was happening to Doc's speech patterns. I decided to pay attention. Doc said, "Have you ever made a normal cast, seen a loop of line buried in the spool, and had to pull off 20 yards of line to get to it?

"That's proof the backlash starts at a point near the axle and moves out. In technical terms, the riga morta forta pin slews the france and hinders reciprocity." He settled back and let go another billowing cloud of incinerated rubber. "That's why I don't use a baitcaster," Doc finished.

I held my breath and peered at Doc through the smoke, wondering if he had slipped on northern slime and landed on his head in the Twilight Zone. Maybe he had breathed too much of the happy gas he gives his dental patients.

Maybe he had breathed too much of the happy gas he gives his dental patients.

Whatever his problem, I decided to sort mine out later. I put the bungled baitcaster rig aside, picked up my open-face jigging outfit, tipped the jig hook with a nightcrawler, and effortlessly cast into the shallows. I slowly worked the jig over a jumble of rocks and sunken tree limbs, hooked a nice walleye, and pulled her in.

Doc volunteered: "I think it's a conspiracy."

"What is?" I asked, admiring my catch before releasing it.

"Backlashes," he said.

"How do you figure?" I anticipated this could be a good one, requiring my full attention. I set my pole aside, poured half a cup of wet coffee grounds, and sat back to listen.

"I read about a study in the National Freshwater Fishing Review," Doc said. "You ever read that magazine?"

"Not recently," I said. "My subscription ran out and I lost the address to renew it." Even though I had never heard of the publication and doubted it existed anywhere but in Doc's mind, I wasn't about to show my possible ignorance or derail his toy train of thought by challenging his alleged source.

"Anyway," Doc continued, "the study found that a professional, and I use that term loosely, bass fisherman will cast and retrieve his baitcaster reel an average of 160 times for each fish caught. Out of that number, two or three casts result in a backlash that can be sorted out within a few seconds. Those backlashes are naturally edited out of TV fishing shows, so fishermen and reel companies won't look bad."

"Naturally," I said. I had read somewhere that deranged people should be humored.

"However," Daffy Doc continued, "after every 5.3 fish caught or after about 850 casts, a granddaddy backlash will occur, severe enough to require cutting at least 10 yards of line off the reel. So, on the average, every 10 fish caught eliminates 20 yards of line. With me so far?"

This was going to be a doozy, even better than the NASA research he told me about at breakfast that proved redheaded women came to Earth from another solar system. I was curious to see where this one was going, so I chewed my coffee and replied, "Yup, Doc, I'm with you."

"For a professional fisherman to lose that much line to backlashes is hard to believe," Doc said. "But an amateur angler loses up to three times as much!" He pounded the boat seat with his fist for emphasis and ran a treble hook from a Dardevle through his flannel shirt sleeve.

As he tried to yank it free, he forged ahead as if nothing had happened. "That means for every 10 fish (jerk!) an amateur catches using a baitcaster reel, he could theoretically lose up to (puuul!) 60 yards of line. If only one million amateurs fish with baitcasters on a daily basis—a low estimate—each would catch an average of 10 fish a day (tug!). That is a line loss of some 60 million yards. Over a year, that's... uh... over 20 billion yards of line to (RRRRIP!) replace."

I was impressed at the assortment of numbers he used to back up his dubious theory and how he managed to keep a straight face through his discourse, even though his shirt sported jagged holes where the lure had ripped out.

"In summary," Doc said, "I think a conspiracy exists between fishing line manufacturers and baitcaster companies to design reels that backlash." Doc's lectures were usually palatable, after a shovel or two of salt, but this time he came off like Deputy Barney Fife playing to me as Sheriff Andy Taylor.

"That's the most ridiculous thing I've ever heard," I said with a hoot, a raspberry, and a few snickers. "Where did you get such nonsense?"

"In the National Freshwater..."

"... Fishing Review," I finished. "That's right next to the supermarket tabloids with stories about Elvis running a taxidermy shop owned by Jimmy Hoffa in International Falls."

Doc puffed his cigar, a faraway look in his eyes, as if trying to remember where he parked his Land Rover after a hard night in Nairobi.

To snap him out of his trance, I asked, "Anything in there about why line gets caught under skirted spools on open-face reels? Or why a piece of toast dropped on the cabin floor always lands buttered side down?"

"Good questions," Doc said, unfazed by my flippancy. "I don't know much about the physics of whole wheat, but I'd guess the added weight of the butter relates to a higher gravity coefficient. On the other hand, I'm somewhat of an expert on spinning reels, which I prefer to use, by the way."

When he picked up his new spinning outfit for show and tell, he accidentally banged it with the end of his cigar. Live ashes burned a hole through his khaki pants. He beat at the sparks in 4/4 rhythm, his voice rising in pitch as he spoke. "In the case of a spinning reel, the spool doesn't move, so any problem is caused by the unequal tension of the line coiled around it. Yow!"

He jumped to his feet, doing an interesting dance as smoke rolled from the vicinity of his right front pocket. Sensing he was in trouble, I dumped what was left of my coffee overboard, scooped up some water and doused the fire before it reached his BVDs. In response, he pulled a Bic out of his life vest, lit what was left of his 'gar, sat down and continued his explanation without missing a beat.

"The line, if installed properly by hand or machine, is wound on the spool at a constant tension," Doc said, chugging away on his 6.75-13 Firestone stogie. "The tension changes dramatically on the first cast, becoming loose on the outer coils and remaining tight on the inside coils.

"Too much line on the reel acts like a spring when the lure hits the water. Boooinnng! It bounces back toward the reel, either wrapping around the release mechanism or roller guide, or slipping under the spool. That's why it's important not to wind too much line on the reel and to control the tension."

"Could you put that in simpler terms, Doc?" I braced myself.

"Of course," he said. "Don't rely on chrome-plated fender dents and rimples to stave off a wheel fracture, unless there's a line-up on the mizzen crank."

Well, that was the back that broke the camel's straw. I fired up the little Evinrude and headed for the cabin.

"Where we going?" Doc asked, hanging on tight as I made a bat turn.

"Back to reality, that's where," I said. "Someplace you haven't visited yet today."

"Did I ever tell you about my trip to Shangrila?" Doc yelled over the motor noise.

"The place hidden somewhere in the Himalayas?" I yelled back.

"No, it's a little barbecue joint outside Davenport," Doc said. "The ribs are paradise."

Next morning, and for the rest of our week-long fly-in stay, Doc was almost back to normal, giving sage advice to me and to the rest of our group on an array of subjects. As far as we can tell, he hasn't relapsed on any of our trips since.

Although I have no formal training in psychology, I figure Doc felt the need to remove an acre or two of silly cells that had accumulated in his brain pan over the years. And he let 'em fly all at once.

In retrospect, I admit the day of lunacy was entertaining, but it goes to show that even a fine fettle has a snitchel fit every now and then. I'm just glad it was him, not me.

Thanks, Doc.

EPISODE 16

If A Picture's Worth 1,000 Words, I Have A Library In My Closet

"Which shelf?" I called to my wife as I opened the door to the linen closet.

"The top one, I think," she answered. Then too late, she screamed, "Be careful!"

If you've ever had the pleasure of taking annual fly-in trips to the Northwest Ontario Bush, loaded to the gills with eighth-ounce jigs and countless rolls of Kodak film, you know what happened next. Down poured a sliding, fluttering, multicolored avalanche of photographs that provided proof of a lifetime of fishing adventures, but in no particular order. On the spot, I decided it was high time to do something about it.

Since I was the trip chairman that year, I phoned Doc, my tooth technician and asked him to bring his fishing photo collection to the upcoming planning session. It was time to put the final touches on the food list and travel plans for our annual Canadian drive-up fly-in. Doc volunteered to call the rest of the group—the policeman, attorney, banker, and plant manager—and ask them to bring their pictures, too.

Thursday night the five men arrived at my house with an assortment of boxes, bushel baskets, grocery sacks, and steamer trunks overflowing with images of paradise. I'd added two extra leaves to the dining room table, but it was still too small to hold the hundreds, no, thousands of photographs.

"Looks like we all have the same problem," I said, stacking my snapshots four feet high in front of me. Many were still in their processing envelopes. "Anyone ever think of buying an album?" I asked.

"I did the first two years," the policeman said, "but never had time to sort through them after that."

"So you have 10 years . . ."

"Eleven."

"Eleven years of fishing pictures you haven't organized?"

"That's about the size of it."

And speaking of sizes, there were 3 x 5s, 5 x 7s, a few 8 x 10s, faded Polaroids with saw-toothed edges, and oddballs that must have been shot with antique Brownies. Most were in color, but a few were black and white, and some could have been either.

"What do we do now?" the banker asked, trying unsuccessfully to peel apart two face-to-face photos that had either spent some time in the La Brea tar pits or at the bottom of a Smucker's jelly jar.

"Let's break out the refreshments and plan the trip," the attorney suggested. "This mess hasn't been a significant priority during the last decade, so I think it can wait a few more minutes."

We all quickly agreed and trooped out to the garage where I kept my trusty little Lund and a rusty old refrigerator. Doc climbed into the boat and gingerly lowered himself onto one of the hard wooden seats. He said he wanted to gradually ease into sitting like that in Canada for six days, 15 hours a day. The banker rocked the boat on the trailer springs to give Doc a more realistic ride, and the attorney produced a good imitation of a 6-horse Mercury at full throttle. One by one we attacked the contents of the refrigerator. Luckily, I remembered to oil the hinges that morning, because it opened and closed with some regularity for an hour or so.

The banker rocked the boat on the trailer springs to give Doc a more realistic ride.

While we wet our whistles and Doc rode the concrete waves, we took care of the more serious business at hand. The previous year's food list had been just about perfect in quantity and variety. We decided, however, to scratch one can of baked beans and the blue cheese dressing in hopes of reducing the frequency and severity of nocturnal flatulence.

The banker volunteered to drive the station wagon he conveniently acquired from one of his customers who had defaulted on a loan, and the plant manager tossed his pickup into the northbound motor pool. The planning business out of the way and our thirsts sufficiently quenched, we reluctantly headed back to the house, leaving behind a cloud of orange smoke from Doc's totally repulsive cigar and a cloud of blue smoke from one of his equally obnoxious jokes.

I secretly hoped a large rodent had crawled up from the basement, carried all the photos back to its lair, and chewed them up while we were outside. No such luck. There they were in all their shutterbug glory.

"Let's begin at the beginning," the policeman said, opening his dusty fat album of first-trip pictures. We gladly left our individual 35mm haystacks, gathering around him as he turned the pages.

The photos were arranged to tell a complete story of the trip, from start to finish. The first was the obligatory group shot taken by one of the wives or girlfriends just before we left. Then one of Knobby Clark greeting us from the front of his fly-in business in Sioux Lookout, and an action shot of us loading the Beaver float plane with our food and tackle.

Aerial views of trees and lakes followed. Then the cabin. Then men riding in boats, catching fish, holding fish, cleaning fish, eating fish, walking to the two-holer, returning from the two-holer, playing cards, and sleeping. Next followed the plane landing for the flight out, aerial views of trees and lakes, and last was the obligatory bearded group shot taken by Knobby just before we headed home.

"Let's compare this one to the second-year album," Doc said, and the policeman put them side by side. The only differences were the cabin, a classic Canadian sunset, Doc lighting one of his sour cigars, and the naked backside of a person taking a bath in the lake.

"What lake is that cabin on?" the banker asked.

"Kezik? Wesleyan? Bamaji? Road House?" the attorney guessed. "It's hard to tell for sure, because Knobby has so many outpost lakes and we try a different one every year."

"Besides that, he's always tearing down old cabins and putting up new ones," the banker added.

"And who do you suppose that is?" I asked, pointing at the au natural bather.

"Beats me," the plant manager said.

"Hummm," Doc mused, studying the photo more closely. "No identifiable marks. You sure that's one of us? He's mighty skinny."

"We've all probably gained a few pounds in the last 10 or 12 years, Doc," I said. "And I'll bet if we dig through our shots, we'll find enough of the same view to provide evidence of our gradual middle-age spread."

Then, bizarre as it seems to me today, we feverishly went to work, sorting out all the rearview bathing photos we could find—41 of them, and we probably missed a dozen or more. Back then, film processing labs didn't stamp the date on the flip side of the prints, so we had no way of knowing what year they were taken. We lined them up on the couch.

After a few minutes of riotous laughter, then an embarrassed silence, I said, "Gentlemen, I vote we destroy these fleshy photos lest they fall into the wrong hands . . . those of our wives."

"I second that emotion," the attorney replied. He was by far the most consistently porky member of the group over the years. "I think I recognize myself in a couple of these, and I'm tired of being the butt of your photographic jokes." With that, he began tearing them into tiny pieces and didn't stop until nary a piece was big enough to incriminate any of us.

We returned to the table and Doc asked, "Do you think it's possible that only one complete set of photos is here and all the rest are duplicates we've made for each other?"

"Sure looks like it," the banker said. "I mean, let's face it, how many ways can you shoot a guy showing off a freshly caught walleye? Only thing that changes is the color of our clothes."

"Not necessarily," the policeman proudly said. He was by far the most consistently in-shape group member. "I've worn the same shirt for 13 years." He pointed to the red and black polyester fashion statement in two of the photos.

"That must be why you never catch any fish over a pound and a half," the plant manager snorted. "Maybe you should wash that shirt sometime. I don't think stinkbait works with walleyes."

While I separated the rowdy boys to prevent damage to my wife's overdecorated dining room, Doc dragged out a handful of fishermen-holding-fish pictures. All the walleyes appeared to be at least three pounds, except those on stringers for feasting purposes, which average an ounce either side of two pounds. The northerns were invariably hogs, or hogettes as the case may be.

"Why do we take the same shots over and over every year?" Doc asked.

"Just lucky, I guess," the plant manager said, then let go a particularly loud belch that knocked over a commemorative Elvis plate in the china cabinet. Much to my regret, it didn't break.

> *The northerns were invariably hogs, or hogettes as the case may be.*

Suddenly, Doc got a great idea. It's not that he changed expression or a tiny light bulb appeared over his head or anything like that. I knew he had a great idea, because he said, "Hey! I have a great idea!"

"What's up, Doc?" I asked. I try to use that Bugs Bunny line whenever possible.

"How valuable are these photos to you guys?" Doc asked, making a sweeping gesture over several house payments worth of colored paper.

"It's not the photos themselves," the attorney said. "It's the memories they represent."

"Exactly," Doc said. "Memories of special moments in the Bush. Good times with good friends."

To illustrate our years of harmony and togetherness, Doc shuffled through the archives and found a shot of the attorney and policeman, their boat hung up on a rock in the middle of the lake, while the banker and Doc hooted at them out of strangle range. Since I wasn't in the picture, I must have captured that one with my camera. But I could swear it had been Doc and me in the beached boat, not Doc and the banker. I guess time, lies, and repeated storytelling make all things possible.

"Give me your photos," Doc said, "and for the price of a nice album and a few dollars worth of duplicating work, I'll come back with a product you'll all be proud of."

The negatives were still in most of the processing envelopes, and Doc said he'd protect them with his life, just in

EPISODE 17

Where There's Smoking There's Fire

Mid-May is when we usually meet to make final plans for our annual first of June drive-up fly-in trip to the walleye wilderness of Northwest Ontario. At that meeting, we plan the trip and renew friendships not maintained during the year. It's also a time of excitement and anticipation. We act like a bunch of four-year-old kids on the way to our first circus.

Although births, deaths, marriages, graduations, and life's other minor interruptions have caused some of us to miss a year or two, we've each made the Canadian trek at least a dozen times, and some of us even more. You'd think we'd know the routine by now, but each year includes a good measure of confusion, as well as the fear that at the last minute, something will go terribly wrong to spoil the trip. The closest we ever came to fishus interruptus was the Year of the Fire.

Doc was group chairman that year, and he was taking it

seriously. We met at his house to decide who would drive and what we should take in the way of pork and beans and onions and toilet paper, not necessarily in that order, but certainly in that logical progression.

After the provisions were settled upon, we proceeded with a round robin show-and-tell of new killer lures, riggings, and related information that would help us catch Mister Monster Walleye.

The banker showed off his new tackle box, so big it needed its own boat. The plant manager tutored us on knot tying. The policeman gave us a sample of the venison sausage he was bringing along to delight our palates. The attorney's Exhibit A was his annual lecture on trolling spoons— silver for sunshine, copper for clouds. And I modeled my new rain gear that featured hermetically sealed seams and arm pits that breathed.

Doc, taking his turn last, made a short speech before unveiling his contribution to the group. "In years past, several negative comments have been directed at the cigars I smoke," Doc said (an understatement, if ever I smelled one). "So I've taken it upon myself to change that perception by laying in a stock of cigars of unsurpassed quality."

Doc placed an old mildewed briefcase on the dining room table. "Gentlemen," he said, "allow your senses to feast on this." He opened the lid and the stench of decomposed civet cat filled the air. As nostrils quivered, eyes watered, and several of us breathed through our mouths to suppress our upchuck reflexes, Doc continued. "These imported cigars are made by expert craftsmen on a small island in the Aegean Sea. They use only the finest wrappers and purest tobacco."

"Isn't the Aegean where Hercules cleaned out all those horse stables?" asked the attorney, wrinkling his nose and making exaggerated shoveling motions.

Before Doc could answer, his wife walked into the room and apologized that the sewer must have backed up again. But when she discovered the source of the odor, she suggested that the alleged tobacco products either be flushed or taken outside. After a brief protest, Doc sadly closed the briefcase and we followed him, just out of nose range, to the screened-in back porch.

"Isn't there a limit on how many cigars you can take across the border, Doc?" the policeman asked, hopeful of a legal obstacle that would either halt the export of the things or trigger an international incident.

"Yes," Doc said, "but split six ways, we're right at the maximum."

"I was afraid of that," I said.

"Anybody want to try one before the trip?" Doc asked.

In unison, we replied, "No!"

To change the subject, the plant manager brought up the question that was wandering around all our minds but was reluctant to sneak out through our voice boxes: "Doc, what about the chance of fire?"

We all knew the road from about Virginia, Minnesota, all the way to Sioux Lookout, Ontario, was hemmed by trees. The winter had been mild with hardly any snow, and without rain the trees and other vegetation were as dry as Aunt Lucy's Thanksgiving turkey.

With a helpless smile and a shrug of his shoulders, Doc said, "I'll call Knobby Clark tomorrow." (We used Knobby's fly-in service out of Sioux Lookout back then, and we still do today.)

Even though it was early and nobody's wife

or girlfriend had phoned with orders to "GET HOME RIGHT NOW!" we shuffled to our cars and rolled slowly away, fearing the worst.

Early the next morning I called Doc's office. He somehow beat his receptionist to the phone.

"Six days and a wake-up," Doc said, instead of hello. His dental drill was whining as one of his patients gurgled for mercy in the background.

"How's it look, Doc?" I could hardly stifle my anxiety.

"Not bad," Doc said. "It's just a small cavity on the occlusal surface of an upper bicuspid. Go ahead and spit."

"Not your patient, Doc," I said. "The trip! How's the trip look?"

"I spoke to Knobby."

"And?"

"The ice has been out for a month and a half, and the water is at least a couple feet low in all the lakes," Doc said. "There's danger of fire everywhere west and north of International Falls, and fires are burning around Kenora and near Red Lake."

"Does that mean the trip's in trouble?"

"Could be. Knobby said to come ahead and hope for the best," Doc said, without a lot of optimism.

I had a free minute or two before writing an ad about a new blue teat dip that controls mastitis infection in dairy cows, a really exciting assignment, so I said I'd pass the word. "What shall I tell the rest of the guys?"

"Brush after every meal and try to floss more often," Doc said.

I hung up before his drill began to sing.

Two weeks later, the Northwest Ontario fires had spread south and east of Red Lake, but had not reached Dryden, where we always stopped for groceries. After a quick conference call to the group and a consensus to go for it, we loaded

> **There's danger of fire everywhere west and north of International Falls.**

up and headed north.

At the International Falls border crossing, we were met by the usual questions. "Where were you born?" "How long will you be here?" and "How much tobacco are you bringing into Canada?" We had rehearsed while waiting in line with about 500 carloads of fishermen from Minnesota, Iowa, Illinois, and the Dakotas. Our answers seemed to satisfy the questioner. Doc, who was behind the wheel, wet his lips in anticipation of diving into his cache of septic tank cigars.

Then she said, "Where you headed?"

"Sioux Lookout to fly in to an outpost cabin," Doc said.

"Oh," she said, soberly. We didn't like the sound of that at all. "When you get across the bridge into Fort Frances," she pointed, "go half a block straight ahead and stop at the Natural Resources office on the right for a permit to travel in that direction."

"Is it bad?" Doc asked.

"It's bad," she said.

We weren't really in the mood to hear that our annual escape to Walleyeland was in jeopardy, especially after a 10-hour drive. But Doc said, "Let's get the permit and see if we can safely get to Sioux."

While the policeman completed the necessary paperwork, Doc called Knobby. No fire in the area yet, but restrictions would be in effect if and when we flew into the Bush.

On the road again, the policeman discussed the situation. Chances of rain were still low, and fire danger was high. Some fires were raging toward Kenora, but many had either been extinguished or burned out.

During the last 20 miles before the road splits and heads northwest for Kenora and northeast for Dryden, we witnessed the destruction. Trees lay like black Pick-up Sticks as far as the eye could see. Here and there a tiny oasis, a circle of green growth, lay unbelievably untouched by the flames. In the center of small lakes, airborne sparks had reduced islands of pines to heaps of ash.

As we witnessed the sad sight, we discussed at length where to find shelter should fire sweep down on our cabin. Obviously not the islands. In an overturned boat on the lake? Would we have enough air to breathe? For how long? It was early June. Would we die of hypothermia in the cold water?

We drove on. Ours was the last vehicle allowed to travel east to Dryden. A barricade was dragged across the intersection after we were told to be alert and not to drive through innocent-looking smoke or flames.

Many more miles of devastation stretched along the nearly deserted highway. To keep out the heavy smoke smell, we rolled up the car windows. But that didn't do much good. When we arrived at Dryden to buy groceries, our clothes smelled like we'd been squatting around a campfire all night.

The drive up to Knobby's was uneventful, and we saw no evidence of fire. Twice the trusty de Havilland was loaded for the fly-in, and twice we had to unload it when fire fighters commandeered the plane for chain saws, shovels, and other gear. Although the delay cut into our fishing time, we grudgingly accepted that their mission had priority over ours.

The Beaver finally returned in late afternoon, took on fuel, and we again loaded our food and gear. Before we boarded, Knobby warned that once we reached the outpost, no variance from the rules established by the Canadian authorities would be allowed.

"First, no shore lunches," Knobby said. "Second, make sure the cabin chimney has a screen in place to act as a spark arrestor. Third, if any member of your group is found responsible for starting a fire in the Bush, all members will remain until it is out and will be assessed the cost of the government's fire fighting effort."

"Is that all?" Doc asked.

"One more thing," Knobby said. "No smoking in the boats or anywhere outside the cabin."

I saw Doc's eyes lose their sparkle and could swear I heard a whimper. All those imported cigars would be restricted to smolder stinkily inside the cabin, not puffed on as he cranked in coveys of walleyes. Not savored on a flat rock after a peanut butter and sweet pickle sandwich. And maybe the most miserable loss of all, no cigar to accompany protracted visits to the two-holer.

For all intents and purposes, Doc is an upstanding, morally responsible guy. He supports community projects with time and money. He belongs to fraternal clubs and professional associations. He pays enough taxes to keep the IRS off his back. He even goes to church with his wife and kids when the weather or a flat tire on his golf cart keeps him off the course.

But he knew deep down that if he took those cigars to the outpost, he wouldn't be able to control his cravings and would smoke them anywhere and anytime he pleased. So in deference to the rules of Bush fires, he removed the briefcase of cigars from the plane and returned all but one to the car.

"Because I can't smoke as I want to in the Bush," Doc said, "and since my heavy smoking in the cabin is not acceptable to your wimpy nasal passages, I will enjoy one cigar right now."

Knobby checked his watch. "This plane has to drop you off and be back before dark," he said. "You have five minutes."

Doc used the time granted as if he were an unrepentant condemned man facing a firing squad. He leisurely examined the 'gar, sniffing it as if it were a slice of Mom's freshly baked apple pie. With a dreamy look on his face, he flicked his Bic with a flourish and set fire to the small brown dirigible.

Any fond memories of apple pie died a tragic death for those of us downwind, assaulted by the smoke. The attorney said the cigar smelled like horse hair held together by Elmer's glue and goat spit. The banker observed he'd been to landfills offering a more pleasant aroma. And the policeman likened the experience to a stroll through the swine barn at the Iowa State Fair.

Five minutes later, when everyone in nose range had suffered enough, Doc stuffed the barely used noxious weed into a bucket of sand and climbed aboard the plane.

Our week in the Bush was outstanding. The low water didn't prevent each of us from catching a zillion good walleyes. We saw the sun every morning and the stars every night. On one or two days we thought we could smell smoke blowing in maybe 50 miles from the northwest, but fire didn't threaten us. On our last day, we were treated to a sunset of magnificent proportions, enhanced by the atomized remains of a few hundred square miles of forest.

But best of all, for six whole days and nights, the incense of onions and garlic and frying bacon, and the pure fresh air of the Northwest Ontario outdoors remained intact.

The year immediately following the Year of the Fire, Doc succumbed to such smoke-filled debauchery that we designated it the Year of the Cigar. But that's another story.

What's important is that for one short week, Doc gave up something he truly loved to save our sensitive noses and possibly a couple million acres of trees. Is he a great guy, or what?

Thanks, Doc.

EPISODE 18

When Dads And Kids Go Separate Ways It Usually Works Out In The End

As much as I enjoy fishing, some years back I spent a week in the Northwest Ontario Bush, and I don't remember catching a single fish. It was the year Dad died.

One afternoon in late May, Mom called me at work. Dad was in the hospital again. I was going to be in town for a dental appointment, so I told her I'd stop by the hospital. When I hung up, I checked the calendar to see if the inconvenience of Dad's illness would interfere with my annual Canadian fishing trip. I was to leave with Doc and the rest of the guys on a Friday, just over a week away, so I figured that was ample time for Dad to get well enough to go home.

I drove to Des Moines, found Dad in intensive care, and visited with him about one thing or another. Of course I expected him to survive yet another setback, and I think he did, too. Even though nine years of drugs and surgery and chemotherapy and prayers couldn't cure him, he seemed as strong as the other times he'd beaten the odds. I told him I'd visit later and drove on out to Doc's for some dental high jinks.

Doc practices dentistry by profession, along with a form of crude psychology on whoever will stand or sit still long enough. I was in for a double dose. With his fingers and what felt like various farm implements banging around my molars, Doc carried on a one-sided conversation about the advantages of jigging plastic grubs as opposed to rigging livebait. Although fishing was on his mind, he knew Dad's health was taking up most of the space in my brainpan. While I rinsed and spat, Doc asked, "So, what's the prognosis?"

"Fifty-fifty," I said, the same answer covering both Dad's chances of survival and if I was going to make the fishing trip.

"Anything I can do?" Doc asked, rummaging in his instrument tray and coming up with what looked like a miniature tire iron.

"Not really, " I replied, eyeing the tool suspiciously. "Even though Dad's a fighter, the surgeon says all his organs are pretty well shot. It's just a matter of time."

"It's just a matter of time for all of us, isn't it?" Doc said.

"Yeh, I guess so," I said, thinking, uh-oh here comes Doc Freud.

"I mean, one way or the other, we're all headed for that perfect drift in the sky." Back then, Doc had a habit of coming up with the corniest metaphors imaginable, and most of them included references to fishing. And he still does it today.

I hated to give Doc an opening for his psychoanalytical babble, but I didn't want to leave him hanging. And deep down, I guess I needed the support. So I said, "You mean death is inevitable, right?"

"Sure as you can catch more fish on light line," Doc said. "How are you holding up?"

"Pretty good," I said, "unless you slip again and snag my

gums with one of your chrome wrecking bars."

"Sorry," Doc said. "My lower unit jumped out of the water for a minute there."

At that point, I could have easily strangled Doc with an imaginary starter rope. But I closed my eyes instead, and while Doc did what he does best, I thought of the few times in my life I had fished with my dad. Evidence of one was a photo taken when I was maybe four, so I can only fantasize about the experience. We were standing with an uncle who lived near Blackduck Lake, up above Bemidji, Minnesota. Dad was holding a northern about as big as I was. The men looked at the camera and smiled. I looked at the fish and cried.

Another time when I was probably eight or nine, I recall fishing with Dad and Grandad for bullheads somewhere near Waterville, Minnesota. I remember we caught dozens of the huge yellow-bellied creatures and that Grandad was using, of all things, a fly-rod. My dad did just fine with a drop line, and I got to use Grandad's extra rig, a brand new Zebco outfit I could cast about a city block. Although I doubt the long-distance presentation was necessary to outwit the species, I demonstrated my expertise every 30 seconds or so, to the obvious discomfort of my more patient fishing companions.

Sometime during my high school days, I asked Dad about the old photo and the bullhead outing and why he didn't fish anymore. He told me he fished more often before the business, four kids, a ham radio, and waxing the Chevy took all his time. He spoke of priorities and responsibilities, foreign concepts to me then, and the subject of fishing was dropped.

We didn't mention it again until four or five years later when I showed him pictures of my inaugural Canadian fly-in trip. It was right after he had his first cancer operation. He listened intently as I told him all about the fish and the fun and the wilderness, and I think I detected a little bit of envy in his eyes. But after a while he switched on the transceiver and called CQ DX for anyone listening in Jordan or Japan or somewhere else in another world. At that time, I figure his priority was staying in touch with his long-distance friends as long as he could, so we put the conversation on hold for another few years.

"That should do it," Doc said, yanking the dental bib from my neck.

"Think I should go?" I asked.

"You'll have to," Doc said. "I have another appointment in five minutes."

"Grrrr. You know what I mean, Doc."

"Well," he said, "if what's bothering you is guilt about going on the trip or about somehow retroactively being a better son, I can't give you any advice to make it go away." Then that strange look crossed his mug again and he said, "Just because one fish is caught, doesn't mean the rest stop biting."

"But doesn't the fish's next of kin lay low until after a reasonable mourning period?" I asked.

"Could be," Doc said. "But not for long. After all, you only swim around once in life, so grab all the baitfish you can."

That sounded vaguely familiar to me, and even made sense, which showed what a bad state my mind was in. So before Doc muddied the water more, I shoved off and motored back to the hospital.

Dad still seemed to be in good spirits, despite the IVs and hospital food. We joked some, and he mentioned my upcoming fishing trip and said not to worry about him, that he'd be fine. Two days later, however, medical complications put an end to his long struggle.

After the memorial service, my lady friend thought it best that I take some time off to regroup. Mom, who was in good hands with my sisters, said Dad knew how much I loved to fish and that I should go to Canada as planned. So I went.

After an all-night drive, our party arrived at Sioux Lookout for the fly-in. There were only five of us that year because the banker's wife stubbornly requested his presence on their first anniversary. Although we counseled a quickie Mexican divorce, true love won and he stayed behind.

The morning was overcast as we loaded our gear into the Beaver and waited for the ceiling to lift. In the meantime, we visited with our favorite fly-in folks, Knobby Clark and his wife Bobbie. They showed us the map of the lake we had chosen for that year's slice of paradise, and my fever was building for wetting a line. Then, one by one, members of my usually abusive and rowdy group cautiously strolled up to me, put on a sorrowful look and said, "How's it going?" I'll admit I choked back some tears at first, but after a few more "How's it goings," I was ready to choke a few fishermen.

I told Doc and the rest that I didn't need sympathy anymore. After all, I was a big boy well over 21 who owned a car and two boats, a set of pots and pans, and most of my hair. They obviously took my not-so-subtle hint, because they reverted to their former obnoxious selves by the time the plane lifted off the water.

Lulled by the drone of the powerful engine, I drifted off to Memory Land, thinking of other long-ago vacations. Until I was about 15, my family camped a week or two every summer on the shore of Mille Lacs Lake, north of Minneapolis. Conditions often were good that time of year for "skip" reception of radio signals from around the world. Dad would spend the better part of every day talking on his mobile ham radio unit. He often tried to interest me in becoming an amateur radio operator, but I had lots more important things to do.

When we were old enough to know better, my older brother and I begged Dad to rent a boat, but he said the big water was too dangerous. We tried fishing from shore a few times, but only caught clams. As often as I watched fishermen at the busy resorts bring in boatloads of lunker walleyes and giant northerns, I didn't fish Mille Lacs seriously until I was almost 30.

The first day in the Bush we realized, that with only five of us, one would have to fish alone while the others paired up. A 14-foot Lund just wouldn't hold a trio and all the rods and rainsuits comfortably, so I volunteered to go solo. I didn't hang around the rest of the guys much, choosing instead to troll out of sight or skim across the lake and find secluded reedbeds or coves. I must have hooked something other than stumps and rocks, but I can't be sure.

That evening, after a freshly caught walleye feast and dish-washing duty, Doc and I went outside and listened to the gulls and loons as they bedded down for the night.

I don't know if it was the despicable stench of Doc's cigar or the swarm of mosquitoes, but something finally drove me back inside. The attorney challenged me to cribbage and beat me six games in a row, including a double skunk. Then four of us tried some quarter poker. In two hours I lost the equivalent of a car payment and all semblance of decorum. The card game was suspended in deference to my ugly luck and uglier mood.

"What's the matter with you guys?" I yelled. "We came here to have some fun! So let's play!" The louder I got, the quieter they became.

The plant manager humored me for a while, then crawled off to bed. Doc and the rest followed at three-minute intervals. I sat at the table and played solitaire, but didn't win at that either. The Coleman lantern was beginning to sputter as dawn began to glow outside. Doc said, "Why don't you get some sleep?" Although I was ready to give him a ration for his fatherly advice, I was too exhausted to fight, so I killed the lantern and slid into my sleeping bag.

When I awoke, the sun was high, and I wasn't. I gassed up my boat and toured about every nook and cranny of the lake before I found the guys. Doc told me he'd jigged a honey hole where he caught at least 30 walleyes in an hour. And the policeman spun a tale about a big northern that danced on its tail and ran away with a $7.95 lure. I listened and tried to be part of the discussion, but I had to force even the most banal response.

Then, out of the blue, Doc asked me, "You ever go fishing with your dad?"

"Some," I admitted. "When I was really little."

"Have a good time?"

"I guess so."

"You're lucky," the attorney said. "I took my boys to the river last summer and almost had to tie the rods to their hands and stake their pants to the ground to make them stay in one place. They were more interested in rocks and sticks than they were in fishing."

"I know all about that," the policeman said. "My youngest dumped my tackle box right off the end of the dock and thought it was the funniest thing ever. How do you explain to a kid that it's okay to spend a small fortune on gas, tackle, bait, and snacks to catch three baby bluegills, but it isn't okay to dump his dad's tackle box into the drink?" He shook his head, perplexed.

You ever go fishing with your dad?

"My daughter thinks going fishing ranks right up there with Christmas morning," the plant manager said. "Only eight years old and won't let me bait her hook. She even likes to use leeches."

"Naaaaa!" the policeman said in disbelief.

"It's the truth! Scares me to death. Outfishes me every time. If she keeps going like this, I bet she'll be the first woman in America with her own TV fishing show." That brought a chorus of laughs, and I managed a smile.

When the noise subsided, he sadly said, "I'm lucky now, but once she discovers boys and cars, I'll probably never get her out in a boat again." We all thought about that for a while. Then Doc lit a cigar that looked like a corncob with a thyroid problem.

"How 'bout you, Doc?" asked the attorney. "Your boys fired up about fishing?"

Doc locked his eyes on mine and said, "Not one bit. If I've tried once, I've tried a hundred times to get them interested in what excites me most. And I'm really disappointed to think they'd rather play catch with their friends than catch a walleye with me. But somewhere down the road, they'll find a special something that drives them at least as much as fishing drives their old dad. And if I raised them right, we'll share some experiences, and then we'll go our separate ways. I hear that's the way it is between fathers and sons."

"And daughters," the plant manager added. "Don't forget daughters."

Doc and the rest must have fished pretty hard the next four or five days, because we ended up bringing out limits of nice walleyes and northerns. Along the way, I managed to win some of my car payment back and even skunked the attorney in an especially thrilling cribbage game that saw him not only tear a deck of cards in half but also eat the five of clubs.

One crystal-clear night—it must have been near the end of our stay—Doc cleaned fish and I took the guts out to a rock across the lake for the gulls. Halfway back, I cut the motor and listened to the stars for a while. The tears rolled heavy and hot down my cheeks, and I had to hang on tight to the side of the boat so I wouldn't float away.

Almost a thousand miles north of my boyhood home, out in the middle of nowhere, I talked to Dad for the last time. I said I hoped he was getting his reward for being a good person and that I'd try to be a good person, too. He told me to enjoy my life to its fullest and never underestimate the power and priceless value of good friends.

Thanks, Dad.
And you too, Doc.

EPISODE 19

Sometimes Memories Make Better Trophies

If the net hadn't been one of those wide-mouth deep sea rigs, Mr. Big would never have made it into the boat. But there he was, in all his slimy glory. Doc's mug sported such a wide, drooling smile that his cigar almost fell out.

"Gacckle, frink, smonster," Doc said.

"You having a stroke, or what?" I asked, trying to sidestep the big pike's thrashing tail.

"Look, ook, ook, ow, wow fish," Doc continued.

I'd seen some outstanding finned creatures yanked out of these Northwest Ontario Bush lakes in years past, but this one was certainly cause for celebration.

"Huffa, huffa, poo," Doc said, his head circled by a cloud of gray-green smoke as he hyperventilated on the stogie.

Who would have thought that hooking a 20-pound-plus pike on an eighth-ounce jig and then bringing him to the boat, very much against his will, on 6-pound line with no leader was even possible?

> *"Ooopa, woopa, whee!" Doc sang to the loons and gulls.*

"Ooopa, woopa, whee!" Doc sang to the loons and gulls. They had heard this song many times before, so they went about their business as if nothing of great importance had happened.

The excitement had obviously been too much for the successful fisherman, so I worked with the needle nose pliers. The small jig literally fell from the toothy jaw. It had been a remarkably short fight, only three runs before I netted him for Doc. The creature just lay there, eyes giving me the once-over. He did a snake slither and shook his huge head a couple times, probably in response to Doc's billowing cigar smoke which was, without reasonable doubt, the worst thing ever to cross my nostrils.

"I can't handle your cigar and your fish at the same time, Doc," I said. "One of 'em will have to go."

As much as Doc hated to do it, he took one last drag and tossed the 'gar hissing into the lake. When he exhaled, the smoke drifting by me smelled like a fire in a stinkbait factory fanned with a handful of burning turkey feathers.

"Wheezel, yuk, and gark," I said. And when I could breathe again, "So, you gonna let him go?"

I may as well have hit my long-time dentist and friend upside the head with the flat side of a splintery oar. His face assumed a look like those rubber-faced folks in supermarket tabloids who have just been released by aliens after a month of interplanetary incarceration on Venus.

"What do you mean, let him go? This baby is trophy material!" Doc screeched, flecks of saliva spattering his life vest.

"I'm taking him home!"

As Doc rummaged through his tackle box and pulled a brand new super-heavy-duty 64-strand polyethylene stringer out of its plastic wrapper, I thought back on all the years we'd fished in Canada.

That first summer we drove into Sioux Lookout, Ontario, when the six of us trooped into the office at Knobby Clark's Fly-In Lodge and Outposts, we were awestruck at the fish hanging on the walls. The dentist, attorney, banker, policeman, plant manager, and I instantly fell into the trophy trap. Walleyes bigger than anything we'd ever dreamed of, lake trout that defied description, and a stunning collection of pike.

We gathered around the biggest pike and gawked. It spanned a good four feet, with jaws able to crush a bowling ball. Razor blade fins, the backbone a steel spring.

As we stood slack-mouthed, fantasizing about landing such a lunker, Knobby completed our licenses. With a little prompting, he told us that over the years, fishermen had taken many trophies from his string of lakes. Then, with a knowing gleam in his eye, he said, "But they didn't take them all." Look out, Loretta, and Katy bar the door. That's exactly what we wanted to hear.

> **We gathered around the biggest pike and gawked.**

As we loaded Knobby's plane for the fly-in, I wondered whether my giant spoons would be up to the task of tackling a trophy. Would my new Heddon Pal rod hold up? And what about my Palomar knot on the heavy steel leader? Would it stand the shock and strain of an attacking fish? Would it hold until I could tire the beast and bring it on board?

I imagined how proud I'd be with my prize beautifully stuffed in an open-jawed fighting position, lacquered and mounted on a piece of gnarled mahogany, displayed on the wall of my den ... if I had a den. Or in my office ... if I had an office.

And then I thought, wait a minute. I didn't even have a

place for a trophy fish. But Doc did. He had a game room in his basement. And there above the couch, within sight of the pool table and washer and dryer, was a spot that cried out for Mr. Big. And Doc swore he'd someday fill the spot.

"Let's get this guy back in the water," Doc said. "They say the longer you keep 'em alive, the more natural they look when they get to the taxidermist."

I thought about that for a while, then offered, "Is that why people at funerals say, 'Doesn't Uncle Fred look natural?' I'll bet if Uncle Fred or this fish had their druthers, they'd prefer the way they look alive."

Doc poked the stringer through the lower jaw, ran the rope through the brass ring at the other end, and pulled it tight. With some difficulty, he held up the fish and looked at me with a Long John Silver squint to his right eye. "You don't think I should have this fish on my wall?" I knew Doc well enough to recognize this as a challenge. He could see I wasn't too hot about trophies and was looking for an argument.

"Go ahead and kill it," I said. "She's your fish."

"She?" Doc asked cautiously.

"Might be. Can you tell a male pike from a female pike?"

"Well . . . "

"Mighty fat stomach. It's early June. Could be a pre-spawn female full of eggs."

"Naaaah," Doc said, looking the fish over for telltale feminine traits.

"How many eggs you suppose are in there?" I pointed at the fish's heavy gut. "Maybe 10,000? Could be even more than that."

"What are you getting at?"

"That's a lot of potential pike to kill for a trophy hardly anyone will see."

"So every other month I'll hang it in the Adel County Courthouse john," Doc said. "Hey! I think this is definitely a male, and I'm going to keep him."

"Like I said, suit yourself. But it seems like a pretty vain thing to do, killing such a fine specimen and hanging it on your wall, just to prove to yourself and visiting in-laws that you did it." I watched Doc loop and knot the stringer in the oarlock, then slide the fish into the water to gently revive it. "In all my years of fishing," I said, "I've never kept a fish for a trophy."

"That's because you never caught one this big," Doc said.

> *The older I get, the more I value all cold-blooded life. Even fish and certain dentists.*

"True," I freely admitted. "When I was younger, I considered fish as a subspecies of the animal kingdom. You catch 'em, cut 'em up, and eat 'em. But the older I get, the more I value all cold-blooded life. Even fish and certain dentists. Trophy hunting doesn't fit anymore."

"I saw you cleaning a covey of walleyes last night," Doc taunted. "Are they a subspecies?"

"You know what I mean, Doc. This lake has about as many two-pound walleyes as Washington, DC has lawyers. Fishermen taking a few thousand a year for feasting won't even put a dent in the population."

"And what if you snag a 14-pound walleye?" Doc asked craftily. "Would you consider building a special room for it?" The pike was coming around as Doc continued aquatic resuscitation.

"A few years ago, yes," I said carefully. "But not now. Of course, I'd burn up two rolls of Kodachrome. And if possible, I'd have Big Wally officially weighed. But then I'd let it go to take its big-fish genetics back to the breeding grounds."

"This fish is going home with me," Doc said, "and that's final." I knew better than to argue anymore. Now it was the principle of the thing, and an act of God would be needed to turn that creature loose . . . or an act of human compassion.

Back at the cabin we admired Doc's fish, and one just a few pounds lighter that the attorney had caught. We not-so-lucky fishermen grabbed our cameras and crowded around like a herd of hungry paparazzi, snapping away from every angle. The attorney's pike had worn itself pretty well out on a dozen runs and was already belly-up. It wouldn't go to waste, however, because he said he'd clean it in the morning before the plane came to fly us back to Sioux.

> The murder weapon was a single-bit axe wrapped in a towel, which he'd use right before the plane landed.

With a good hour or two of daylight left, Doc took a boat a few miles down to the main camp to ask the resident caretaker how to get a fish ready for "trophyizing." Thanks to Doc's bragging, word of the big fish got around fast, and that evening about dark, two boatloads of fishermen asked to see it. Doc held it up in their flashlight beams, basking in the oohs and aahs of collective congratulations. Doc's pike kicked and jerked as it hung from the stringer.

"Careful, Doc," I warned. "That stringer will break and your trophy will be on its way to Freedom City."

"You'd like that, wouldn't you," Doc said, half joking, but only half.

"Not so much as the fish would like it," I said. "You still have time to release it."

"Fat chance," Doc said.

The next morning, Doc was making preparations for killing and preserving his treasure for the trip home. The murder weapon was a single-bit axe wrapped in a towel, which he'd use right before the plane landed. Just a gentle tap to the skull, then a fast wrapping in plastic to lessen distortion from the death throes. The other members of the group were silent as they watched. Even Doc seemed unusually morose.

"Gonna kill him with kindness, huh, Doc?" I asked.

Doc ignored my sarcastic protest by lighting up one of his rubber-boot cigars and heading to the dock to take another look at his fish. More fishermen from a faraway outpost had heard of the catch, and he held the horse up to be whistled at and even videotaped as it danced on the end of its rope.

Awhile later, the attorney had sharpened his knife and was all set to make fillets out of the other huge pike. As I joined him at dockside to give moral support, we were amazed to see that the hog had righted itself and was showing every sign of survival.

"You sure you want to kill that fish?" I asked. The look on the attorney's face belied his reluctance, especially after watching Doc plan to do the same to his fish, in a more deliberate, but less bloody manner.

"You think he'll make it?" he asked.

"Could be. Pull the stringer out and see," I suggested. After resting for a few minutes under the dock, a gentle prod from an oar sent the second-best pike of the trip meandering off toward deep water with strong, regular tail strokes. The broad smile on the attorney's face turned into a look of despair as he heard the approaching plane.

We all knew what was going to happen next. On the way to the cabin to begin carrying our gear down for the fly-out, I passed Doc and his velvet axe. Our eyes met for an instant, and Doc's seemed to plead for a stay of execution, but I couldn't be sure.

I waited in the cabin and swept the same square foot of floor until I figured it was all over. I had a feeling of shame, maybe guilt that I couldn't quite come to grips with. It was like my brother was being punished for something we'd both done, but I hadn't been caught.

And then the policeman walked through the door and said, "Doc's fish is gone."

I looked up and said, "The stringer broke." It wasn't a question, but a statement of presumed fact.

A nod. "Rope snapped at the brass ring."

"Is Doc shattered?"

"What do you think?" the policeman said. It almost sounded like an accusation, but not quite.

"That's too bad," I said, and I think he was convinced I

meant it.

I went down to the dock to find the banker and plant manager looking out at the deep brown water. The attorney was peeking under the boats, just in case. Doc just stood there, the blue-and-white polyethylene rope hanging limply like a string of rosary beads in his fingers. He watched me approach. I looked him in the eyes a long time before I said, "I'm sorry, Doc."

He shook his head, turned away, and didn't answer, but I have a feeling his voice would have cracked from emotion if he had. What kind of emotion, I'll never know. Even the best of friends have moments that stay forever unshared, and this was one of those moments.

I was at Doc's about two months after we returned to our families and jobs that year. He asked me to follow him down to his game room. There, under a spotlight, above the couch, and within sight of the pool table and washer and dryer hung a small, gnarled mahogany plaque. Mounted on it were an eighth-ounce jig with a bent hook, the frayed end of a new stringer, and a photo of a grinning Doc holding onto a very lively Mr. Big.

I stepped closer to read the brass plate nailed to the bottom. Etched was the date the picture was taken, the weight of the fish (which had already grown to 24 pounds), and these words: The Memory Didn't Get Away.

In all the years since that one, we've often come close to catching trophy-size fish in the Ontario Bush. A few big pike have been coaxed into our nets, and lots of good walleyes. But not once has my friend even hinted that I may have sabotaged his stringer to rob him of his trophy. And for that, Mr. Big and I have only one thing to say.

"Thanks, Doc."

EPISODE 20

Even An Ecoslob Can Clean Up His Act

The shoreline of the pristine Canadian lake snaked slowly ahead as our little Lund rippled the glassy surface. Slabs of rock that sported splotches of orange and blue-gray lichen rose from the shore like petrified humpbacked whales. Occasional shallow coves boasted new quills of spring green reeds. And ragged pines, scrub brush, and a scattering of wildflowers sprouted from the spongy moss-blanketed earth farther inland. If we hadn't fished the same lake 10 years earlier, it would have been easy to imagine we were the first white men to view its untrampled majesty.

The setting was the first week of June, a dozen or more years ago. Doc and I were in a trolling mood, lazily searching for yet another walleye honey hole. Alongside a towering rock wall, Doc pulled in a nice walleye on his #3 Professor spoon. I killed the engine so we could drift and jig for more.

We must have been right in the middle of not just a school, but a major coed college of 3-pound fish, because we hauled in a dozen each before the action stopped flat. I fired up the engine and we moved on. Doc tossed out his Professor again, and holding the rod between his knees, lit a cigar. I braced myself as his first puff of smoke stumbled my way, clung to my life vest like a drowning man, then let go and fell behind, swirling menacingly into what was no longer virgin air.

"New brand of cigar?" I choked. "Smells a little different than yesterday. Like a cross between a cow pie and Irish setter sweat."

"It is kind of special," Doc replied with a grin. "But it's not a new brand, just aged longer."

"Where was it aged? In the Vikings' locker room?"

Doc took another drag, and I ducked to dodge the monstrous smoke that assumed the shape of a ghostly Godzilla as it passed. "Want one?" he offered.

"No thanks," I said. "I'll wait for the movie."

While Doc caught and released a few water-skiing axhandle pike, I expertly skirted the sudden boulders that dotted the points. We were in no hurry. The cool water, colored brown by minerals and plankton, was still clear. I watched clouds of minnows scurry to safety as the shadow of the bow covered them.

What fun. What relaxation.

"What's that?" Doc yelled. I threw the engine into neutral and followed the bent pole to the end of his line where a black and slimy and downright disgusting thing sludged up from the depths.

"Biggest leech I ever saw," I gasped. Then, on closer inspection, "I think it's a wing tip. About a size 11. Why do you suppose a shoe was dumped here in the Bush?"

"No idea," Doc said. "I didn't expect this place to be as pure as it was 10 years ago, but this is ridiculous."

"What are you going to do with it?" I asked, as Doc freed the treble hook from the leather upper.

"Take it back to the cabin, I guess," he said. "Don't want to leave it out here for someone else to snag." And he hung it over an oarlock to drip dry.

"Suppose there's another one down there?" I asked, peering over the side.

"I'm a dentist, not a shoe salesman," Doc said. "But I doubt they would fit you, even if you managed to hook the other one."

"I could wear two pairs of socks," I said. "Or maybe I could stuff some newspaper in the toes."

Instead of dignifying my comments with a response, Doc conjured up another cigar fog that reeked like a Siamese hairball. I put the engine in gear and throttled up to outrun the clawing stench.

Able to breathe again, I speculated, "The shoe probably didn't fall from a passing airliner. Not too many politicians come this far north to sell their soles." The verbal double dribble was met by not so much as a snicker on Doc's part, so I moved on. "And it didn't walk here by itself. So it must have been brought to this spot on purpose. I can't imagine what kind of person would do that."

"You'd never dump foreign matter in the water, would you?" Doc asked slyly.

"Not a chance," I said.

"It's just plain stupid, isn't it?"

"Sure is," I said, realizing too late I had taken the bait and swallowed it down to my kneecaps.

"Obviously, you don't remember the first years we flew up here with our cases of cans with the revolutionary and convenient pull-tab tops."

"I guess I have a vague memory of that," I said, guilt beginning to wash over me like sour milk over a bowl of Cheerios.

"And what did you do with those pull-tabs out here in the boat?" Doc asked. "Take them home to make a chain to hang from your rearview mirror?"

"No," I confessed, "I guess I tossed them over the side."

"You and I and about a thousand other fishermen," Doc said. "And the caps from bottles, too."

I could see the bottle caps in my mind's eye—a brief splash, then fluttering out of sight into the dark waters of fish-filled lakes of long ago. I closed my eyes and saw a flaming condo in Polluters' Hell with my name on the mailbox.

"The steel ones may be pretty well rusted away after 10 years," Doc continued, "but I'll bet the aluminum ones will be around until the Cubs win the Series."

"I get your point, Doc," I said, knowing this lake bottom was stuck with all those aluminum tabs and caps throughout eternity.

"I don't feel very good about all the filter cigarettes I threw overboard, either," Doc confessed, "when I still smoked those foul things."

I couldn't imagine anything fouler than the smoldering abomination Doc held between his thumb and forefinger, but I reserved my comments when I saw he was on an ecological roll.

"Trouble is, we figured a few pieces of shiny metal on the bottom wouldn't make a whit of difference in this vast wilderness," Doc said. "And think of the hundreds of spoons and leadhead jigs we've lost to snags and fish over the years. But we aren't the only people who use this area. Besides the Indians who live in this part of Canada, Knobby Clark has been flying parties of fishermen like us from Sioux Lookout into his outposts for 20 years or more. It's amazing how few signs of man's inhumanity to nature we see."

"Other than every now and then when we hook what appears to be a cordovan Florsheim," I added, the soggy leech-like shoe still dripping into the bottom of the boat.

"You have to admit that a lot of things have been done to protect the environment from thoughtless slobs like we used to be," Doc said.

"Like putting a hefty deposit on bottles so we'll return them," I said. "Or compelling us, for convenience and economic reasons, to switch to cans."

"And pull-tabs that stay on the cans," Doc said. "That was a huge advancement."

I thought about the sad once upon a time when product packaging was as indestructible as we imagined the environment to be. But manufacturers and consumers finally began to understand the importance of reusable or biodegradable containers, and recycling those that nature couldn't quickly absorb.

"Remember when I took my sons, kicking and screaming, to the Boundary Waters a few years ago?" Doc asked.

As I recalled, Doc's kids harbored a strong belief that a brush with nature at the Minnesota-Canada border was not a good way to spend a whole week of their summer vacation. "Didn't you talk them out of taking in a truckload of Coke?" I asked.

"Incredible, but true," Doc said. "They couldn't begin to understand the Boundary Waters rules, and that the only way to preserve the area was by not taking anything in that you didn't also take out. They said, 'C'mon, Dad, what's a little glass or aluminum going to do to such a big place?'

> *They began to appreciate that even a single bottle cap meant someone sometime had refused to respect the rights of others who wanted to enjoy a relatively untouched part of the great outdoors.*

"But after a few days, they began to appreciate that even a single bottle cap meant someone sometime had refused to respect the rights of others who wanted to enjoy a relatively untouched part of the great outdoors. Before the week was over they were like Navy recruits at boot camp, policing the water and camping areas for anything that didn't grow there naturally. Their pockets were jammed with gum wrappers that only a week before they would have uncaringly tossed to the winds."

"So they learned a lesson many kids never learn."

"I hope so," Doc said. "But it's too bad so many Americans have never seen a place that hasn't already been trashed. They think of potato peels and milk jugs floating in a Mississippi backwater as a natural phenomenon. They think beaches made unswimmable and lakes made unfishable by raw sewage, industrial wastes, and agricultural chemicals are an inescapable ingredient of an industrialized economy and are to be expected."

"Can't we turn it around?" I asked, hopefully.

"You ever been to Washington, DC?" Doc asked, looking his toxic cigar in its glowing eye.

"Never had the pleasure," I said.

"I hope it's not an indication of what the federal government thinks about the environment," Doc said, bitterly. "You wouldn't believe the garbage in the streets that surround the Capitol of the richest, most powerful, most educated nation on the planet."

Doc took an angry drag on his cigar and I got a good idea of what the halls of Congress must smell like.

> *Doc took an angry drag on his cigar and I got an idea what the halls of Congress must smell like.*

"I'm sure many socioeconomic excuses justify it," Doc said. "But people who see no reason to clean up the streets where they live and work certainly can't be expected to treat a place they visit any differently."

We were silent for a while. Then Doc heaved his lure overboard and we continued our quest for unsuspecting clusters of walleyes that I hoped were not being distracted by people pollution.

Late that afternoon, as we cleaned enough two-pounders for our evening meal, I asked the other members of our group if they'd seen changes since our stay 10 years earlier. The policeman said he thought the fishing was better. The plant manager couldn't see much difference. The banker said the grouse thumpings were louder. And the attorney surprised me by asking, "Isn't the whole area cleaner than it used to be?"

"How do you figure?" Doc asked, expertly slicing the last tiny bones from a walleye fillet.

"Back then, we left our cans and bottles at the cabin instead of flying them out with us as we do now," the attorney said. "Looks to me like someone has done a good job of picking up the place."

"Maybe Canadian litter laws changed," the policeman said.

"Maybe the bears were tired of cutting their noses on our pork and bean cans," I suggested.

"Maybe the moose carried the junk to a landfill," the banker said.

"Maybe we are trying to erase our footprints," Doc said cryptically, swatting a mosquito as big as a blue jay, coating his neck with a smear of blood that was part his, part walleye.

"Some of us leave bigger footprints than others," the plant manager said, not quite as cryptically, stomping a can flat and tossing it into a fly-out pile with more just like it.

"I don't consider myself an ecology wrecker," I said. "To coin a word, I'm not an ecoslob like some fishermen I know." When Doc gave me a threatening look, punctuated by the dripping blade of the fillet knife, I added, "Present company excluded, of course."

"When we get to a certain age," Doc said, "we want things to be like they used to be; like the good old days. It makes us feel younger and helps us believe that we can be immortal."

Doc was and still is the Old Man of the group, so we turned our attention to his wisdom, even though his credibility was tarnished a bit when he scratched under his nose and left a mustache of walleye guts.

"I don't believe we can ever reverse what civilized man has done to his environment, but we can try to preserve places like this for generations to come." Doc made a sweeping gesture and the fish fluids he flung made an interesting pattern on the front of my white T-shirt.

"Like fishing line," Doc said. "We have to stop throwing monofilament line into the water when we snip the ends from knots or cut off tangles from backlashes. That stuff is almost forever. It won't disintegrate until the time one of us writes the Great American Novel."

Since I make my living writing, the members of the group looked in my direction knowingly and agreed that the mono would be around a very long time, indeed.

"Put the line in your pocket to toss into the trash when you get back to the cabin," Doc said. "It's a simple antipollution procedure that will keep this fishing factory that much cleaner."

Doc finished his butchery, rinsed his knife and said, "How about if from now on we carry a garbage bag in the boat and pick up any trash we see? Maybe when other groups see how uncontaminated the place is, they'll be more inclined to leave it like they found it."

Without discussion, we agreed.

To this day, we continue our litter patrols in Canada, as well as on the lakes, rivers, and farm ponds we fish closer to home. We still find cans, bottles, Styrofoam bait containers, and other refuse at our favorite fishing spots. But as we stuff them into our onboard garbage bags, it seems there's not nearly the amount of 10 or 15 years ago.

This year we're planning our third visit to the lake where Doc caught the shoe. When it dried, he nailed it to the cabin wall with a note reminding other fishermen to help keep the environment clean. Maybe we'll find the wing tip's mate. I realize it won't fit me. But my friend has made me more aware than ever before that it doesn't fit the bottom of the lake, either.

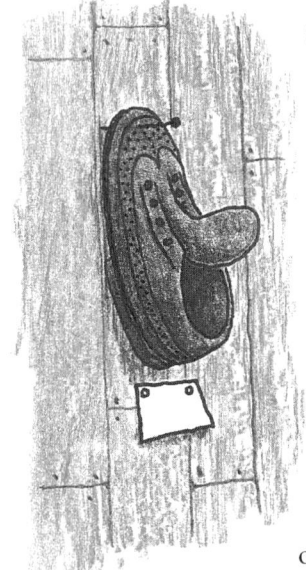

Thanks, Doc.

EPISODE 21

Sometimes The Northwest Ontario Bush Can Be Colder Than Aunt Lucy's Green Bean Casserole

On the first of June, we left Des Moines in a predawn fog, crossed the border at International Falls, stopped in Dryden for groceries, and were greeted about noon in Sioux Lookout by snow flurries. We changed into our long underwear and insulated coats, preparing for the worst. Knobby Clark supervised the loading of his Beaver float plane for the eventual splashdown on one of his outpost lakes.

"How cold's it been, Knobby?" Doc asked, as he snapped fresh 9-volt batteries into his electric socks. Doc's business involves taking large sums of money from the dentally deficient. He can drill away on festering cavities, not bothered in the least by screams and the smoke from burning enamel, but when it comes to temperatures below 40°F, Doc's a basket case.

"A real heat wave," Knobby answered. "After a winter low of minus 62°F, temperatures have stayed above freezing since ice-out, almost three weeks now."

"But last year was 85°F and sunny," Doc whined, stamping his feet to stay warm. I recalled the steamy night a year earlier when a mosquito carried a can of pork and beans almost out the cabin door before the policeman using a series of kung fu kicks drove it away. The beans had to be destroyed.

"That was unusual," Knobby said. "But don't worry. The cold won't affect the fishing, and the new wood stove in your cabin will keep you warm.

"Wood's already cut," Knobby continued, "and as usual, each cabin is equipped with a new ax should you need to cut more."

By 2 o'clock, the sky had brightened enough for Knobby to gain clearance from the local airport for our one-hour flight. After a surprisingly smooth landing on the choppy lake, we taxied in and lashed the port pontoon to the dock. Then we unloaded our gear and stowed it in the cabin.

The policeman and I knocked an inch or two of ice from the decks of our three Lunds, topped off the tanks, and warmed up the brand new Mercs. The plant manager, who preferred his mini chain saw to Knobby's ax, cut enough wood to fire the Queen Mary for at least six transatlantic crossings. The banker stacked the wood in neat piles and carried some inside to dry. Meanwhile, Doc boiled coffee on the propane stove, and the attorney filled the Thermos bottles.

Although late afternoon brought an overcast sky, we still had enough light to fish by, so an hour after our arrival, we were angling for supper. Doc sat in the bow of my boat, an iguana-green cigar jammed into the hole surrounded by his sweatshirt hood. His Bic flared and an instant later a cloud of putrescence the size and shape of the Goodyear blimp appeared. On second thought, it looked more like the Hindenburg.

"Oh man," I protested. "Isn't the weather miserable enough without lighting that skanky thing?"

"I tawdid woodeep my wips wam," he mumbled numbly. "I wood wong."

Every exhale hung on the icy air and mingled with engine exhaust to form a fog bank that trailed our movements along rocky points and drop-offs. Luckily, we'd rigged our rods and tied knots back at the cabin, because our exposed cold fingers were becoming useless.

Doc jigged a grape-colored split-tailed twister of some kind and I bounced a fat crawler over the rocky bottom. In less than 45 minutes, we each boated a dozen nice walleyes, but the excitement that had warmed our hands was wearing off. Unhooking and releasing our catches became more and more difficult. Our Thermos of coffee didn't help much either, because Doc had forgotten it back at the cabin.

"I tawdid woodeep my wips wam," he mumbled numbly. "I wood wong."

Light rain began to fall, blessedly extinguishing Doc's reptilian stogie. When the rain abruptly changed to sleet, we reeled in, motored over to the other boats, made sure we had enough keepers to eat, and headed for home.

For some reason, probably mental instability brought on by the early stages of hypothermia, I volunteered to clean the fish. Since feeling had almost deserted my digits, I wore a steel mesh glove on my fish-holding hand, managing to cut only the fish without too many nicks in the blade of my fillet knife.

By the time I brought my chattering teeth inside our 6-man log cabin, the other guys were beginning to strip off layers of clothing. Darkness had fallen sharply along with the mercury. Coleman lanterns had warmed the air to about 45°F, a good temperature, according to Doc, for cheap white table wine. Shivering like a scared puppy, Doc unscrewed the bottle top, pouring wine into his glass and an equal amount onto the table.

Doc's fire in the new stove standing in the center of the floor was beginning to put out heat. I hadn't seen a stove quite like this one. Its heavy gauge steel frame supported an oval top and bottom and rested on four sturdy feet. It stood about two feet wide, three feet long, and maybe a foot and a half deep. A sliding lid on the top covered a 10-inch opening for adding wood, and a damper wheel with triangle holes in the lower front regulated the draft. A tin pipe about eight inches in diameter reached from the top of the stove and through the ceiling 12 feet above. After the fire really got going and Doc had added a log or two, the place became downright toasty.

The plant manager who had chef duties the first night created a meal of beans with onions, lettuce salad with onions, onion flavored potato chips, and batter fried walleye fillets smothered in onions. After he ate the leftovers, we cut cards to determine bunk assignments. Doc drew a king and claimed the bed closest to the stove. The plant manager drew a queen for second choice, but we insisted that he bed down in one of the boats. As a compromise, he agreed to sleep by a partly open window.

Before lights out, four of us played a few games of pitch while the other two punished the cribbage board. The day had been long, so we quit early and prepared to turn in. One by one we doused lanterns. Through the front window I saw stars emerging from a now cloudless sky.

I brushed my teeth, undressed, and as much as I hated to, I slipped on flip-flops, grabbed my flashlight, and made a frigid visit to the two-holer out back. While I was out, Doc fed the stove a couple logs. He adjusted the damper to barely draw, to keep the fire burning slowly, putting out heat all night. When I returned from nature's call, everyone was in the sack, so I cut the last lantern and tightly zipped up my sleeping bag.

Sometime during the night, I felt cold. Maybe the draft from the plant manager's window was flowing over me. Anyway, I shuffled to the stove and saw by the beam of my flashlight that the fire was hardly burning. I opened the lid and jammed in a few logs, but after a minute or two, it still wasn't burning well. Some dummy had closed the damper almost all the way. When I opened it as wide as it would go, the wood caught fire in a flash. As the heat began to build, I slid the lid closed and crawled back into bed.

I'd been asleep for maybe five minutes when I awoke to what I hoped was a bad dream that included a steam locomotive rumbling past my bed. I sat up to see not the 5:15 from Mason City but the stove, dancing around the cabin. It jumped up and down on the floor with a CHUFF! CHUFF! CHUFF!

Flames shot from the damper opening. The whole thing glowed cherry red from the bottom to about halfway up the chimney pipe. I was fighting to unzip my sleeping bag zipper when Doc let out a roar and rolled away from the bucking monster, upsetting his bed and waking up the rest of the group.

The cabin pulsed with the stove's red glow as the CHUFF! CHUFF! CHUFF! continued. (At the inquest conducted by the attorney the next day, we figured the wood was burning so furiously that it periodically ran out of oxygen and had to suck air alternately down the pipe and through the damper, causing the steam engine effect.)

> **The cabin pulsed with the stove's red glow as the CHUFF! CHUFF! CHUFF! continued.**

By the time Doc escaped from his scorched bedding, I reached the business end of the bellowing inferno, grabbed a broom, and closed the damper down tight. As the fella said the day after Abe Lincoln went to see a play at Ford's Theatre, "That was not a very good idea."

Instead of going out or cooling down, that heat was trapped, making a sound like a chorus of garters snapping at a fat lady circus.

The fire sure didn't behave the way I thought it would, but what to do next? The cabin was lit from the fire as Doc lunged for the broomstick I held.

First, he opened the damper all the way, and the stove resumed its noisy Bunny Hop, causing two of my fellow fishermen to run for safety into the great outdoors. The open door let in a few hundred cubic yards of cold air that the stove appreciated. It jumped even higher off the floor. Knobby had sure done a good job fitting the stovepipe sections, because they somehow flexed and stayed together.

Then Doc slid the top of the stove open to let in even more air. I braced myself for the explosion, or at least to be vaporized by the heat, but the stove immediately stopped dancing, and the roar of burning combustion gases going up the pipe replaced the locomotive noise. Even though the fire burned more violently than ever, the pipe gradually lost its red glow, and the stove began to cool down.

It soon became clear that Doc knew exactly what to do. He barked an order at the policeman and attorney to get a couple buckets of water ready, just in case. And he sent me to round up the rest of the group and make a thorough check of the cabin roof and the surrounding trees and foliage. No sparks were going through the screened chimney cover, and the roof and ground were still wet from the rain and sleet, so we concluded that none of the fire had made its way outside.

After the stove began functioning normally, Doc gave the "all clear" and said we should try to get some sleep. That wasn't within the realm of possibility for me, so I dressed and stood watch until the guys rolled out sometime after dawn.

My lack of knowledge about wood stoves had almost caused a disaster. I caught a razzing—and rightly so—from everyone for placing them in danger. Everyone but Doc, that is.

When I asked him why he was letting me off the hook so easily, he told me about the time he had done about the same thing on a smaller scale when he was a kid. He was sent outside to burn the trash. Using a whole box of kitchen matches when only one would have done the trick, he and his family and the rural fire department spent the rest of the day hosing and stomping out a fire that blackened a garden and a 10-acre pasture.

"Did your folks make it tough on you?" I asked.

"They did for a while," Doc said, "but I found out from my granddad that my dad almost burned down the barn trying to light a kerosene lantern. And my mom started a kitchen grease fire that her mother put out with baking soda."

"In other words," I said, "nearly everybody has had a close call with fire."

"Probably," Doc agreed. "Except most of us were lucky enough to have someone nearby to save our bacon from frying. After my own experience, I learned to handle fire more carefully and to take absolutely nothing for granted when operating a wood stove or even my fireplace at home."

In the days that followed, a rapid warming trend made fishing more comfortable. The sun shone brightly every day, and a few of us even took off our shirts to get a head start on summer tans. About the end of the week, after an evening meal of onions with baked walleye on the side, we gathered around while Doc dug into his bag of medical tricks.

"I've taught you all I know about wood burning," he said. "Heartburn and sunburn must be next."

As he handed out the Rolaids and Solarcaine, we groaned,

"Thanks, Doc."

EPISODE 22

Nightmare On Walleye Street

Judy. I'm not kidding. Judy. That's what Doc calls the mythical walleye who waits only for him, somewhere beneath the dark waves of a Northwest Ontario lake.

Every year, a month or so before our June 1st fishing trip, Doc rekindles his unrequited love affair with Judy. And although others in the group think he should seek professional help for his obsession, I see Doc for exactly what he is, a wild-eyed, raving, get-the-rubber-room-ready, absolutely certifiable banana brain. With intensive therapy including bowling, 32-ounce Black Russians, and rat skin cigars, when you see him on the street, it's hard to separate him from nearly normal people like you and me.

During my annual chew checkup a few years ago, Doc hovered above me with his instruments of mass destruction. Unfortunately, he found a sink hole the size of Ohio in one of my molars. And since a small ant would have no trouble stepping over my pain threshold, Doc administered a few cubic yards of ha-ha gas on top of local Novocain. While we waited for my head to turn to wood, he spoke feverishly about his dream fish.

Doc's new dental technician walked in just in time to hear me mumble, "Is she pretty?"

"Judy is beautiful beyond belief," Doc said. "A smooth fat tummy, sparkling white teeth, and a perfect tail that sways from side to side even when she's standing still."

The dental tech dropped my x-rays on the floor and stared at Doc in shock. "B-b-but your wife's name is Janis."

"Judy's a walleye," I told her, rolling my eyes and trying to indicate that Doc's mind had taken flight through the hole in the ozone layer.

Before she sidestepped from the room, stomping on my x-rays in the process, she gave Doc a look that said, "If this guy actually has the hots for a fish, I'd better get my resumé ready."

"Deep green skin and eyes to get lost in," Doc moaned.

I heard a gasp and then a crash as a tray of plaster smiles destined for a denture maker shattered on the floor.

"How big is she this year?" I asked, knowing Doc's fantasy fish had passed 10 pounds three years earlier and was probably just shy of a short ton by now.

"Lots to love," Doc said, arranging a pipe wrench and a ball peen hammer in his instrument tray. "Right at 14 pounds and a belly full of fire. I'll bet Judy gives birth to 60 thousand kids this spring."

I heard a whimper from the next room and a door slam. I figured Doc would be running an ad for a dental technician when we returned from Canada.

I'd known Doc a long time (some might say too long), so I

realized the finned female figment of Doc's imagination was his way of keeping his oars in the water until we were well on our way to Sioux Lookout. Like the rest of us—the banker, attorney, plant manager, policeman, and me—Doc's hooks had been sharpened and his clothes packed for at least a month. Once we arrived at one of Knobby Clark's outpost lakes, Doc usually forgot about Judy. Not this time.

We were the first party to fish the lake after ice-out. Knobby said we'd be able to catch all the walleyes we could handle only 100 feet from the cabin, a new A-frame on a tree-lined rocky point just below a small rapids. He was right.

The second day, in anticipation of fishing a narrow outlet an hour from the cabin, we packed plenty of eats. After beaching our boats, we sprawled on a slab of smooth rock for shore lunch. As the policeman handed out bologna tripledeckers, vinegar potato chips, and apples, we stripped off our life vests to soak up some sun while we ate. The conversation centered around what you'd expect from a bunch of guys basking in an idyllic fishing paradise—women.

"I'm not completely sure," the attorney said, "but I do believe blondes have the most will power."

"Why?" the banker asked, digging into the chips with a northern-slimed fist.

"Well, I've never had a date with one, which must mean they have the strength to resist a handsome brute like me."

"Good point," the plant manager said, "but what about your experience with brunettes?"

"Never had much luck with them, either," the attorney admitted, a slice of dill pickle stuck to a gob of mustard on his chin.

"I can't imagine why," the policeman said.

"Redheads are my favorite," I said. "In fact, I like them so much I married two . . . one at a time."

> *The conversation centered around what you'd expect from a bunch of guys basking in an idyllic fishing paradise—women.*

"And how about you, Doc?" the banker asked, now eating with his other hand because the chips were tasting a bit too fishy.

But like the excuse politicians use to deny responsibility for their actions on Capitol Hill, Doc was outside the loop. He'd moved to the water's edge, opened his tackle box, and was tying something onto his heavy duty rig. I put a finger to my lips to silence the guys and slipped behind Doc to see what he was doing.

Anyone who fishes knows that fish are sometimes less than picky about what they'll bite. During indiscriminate feeding frenzies, I've caught them on everything from a can opener with dual propellers to a bent nail baited with a sweat sock. But Doc had made a trip to LaLa Land for this number. He turned, a cigar clenched tightly in his teeth, and smiled crookedly at me as the lure swung in the soft breeze. As he braced himself to cast into the depths, the moment hung frozen in time, the lure poised in mid-fling.

At the bottom of the lure hung a chrome-plated treble hook almost as big as my fist. The hook held the toe of a woman's size 7AA high-heeled shoe, not one you'd find at a mall, but at a country craft boutique for the criminally cute. More glass beads adorned that shoe than Peter Minuit gave the Indians for Manhattan Island—green and iridescent blue, gold and silver sparkling in the sun, and running through them, a swirl of puffy purple paint. A couple chicken feathers swept up gracefully from each side. Doc heaved the mess far out in the lake, attracting a swarm of gulls and sending a herd of moose crashing through the underbrush.

The shoe remained afloat for a moment before it bubbled beneath the slick water, stern first, like a torpedoed warship. After a few seconds, Doc began a deathly slow retrieve, puffing on his cigar at each revolution. The smoke was smelled in downtown Duluth and seen from as far away as Winnipeg.

I expected uncontrolled laughter from the other guys, but they sat quietly eating, as if Doc were working a jig and crawler. And Doc chanted, "Judy! Judy! Judy!" as he reeled in the shoe.

At first I thought of Goober's ridiculous impression of Cary Grant on the Andy Griffith Show, but then the real meaning hit me. Cinderella's slipper! The slipper Doc was trying to entice Judy into biting on so he could be her prince and live happily ever after in a fishing paradise.

All at once Doc let out a whoop, set the hook, dug his heels into a crevice in the rock, and cranked for all he was worth.

Every few seconds Judy made a run. And the singing drag sounded familiar, much like a high-speed dental drill. Doc hauled on the rod, trying to overwhelm the giant creature on the end of his line. How big would the fish have to be to get its teeth over that shoe? I stretched my mouth as wide as I could as I pondered its size.

Closer and closer Doc coaxed his quarry, skillfully applying pressure with his rod tip, not letting up for an instant.

"Thar she blows!" Doc yelled, as a huge dorsal fin broke the surface, followed by the sweep of a powerful tail. Then it was gone in a swirl of blackness as the drag sang again.

"You need help, Doc?" I shouted, my question almost drowned by the incessant scream of the reel.

"The net! Get the net!" Doc bellowed.

I rushed to the nearest boat and grabbed a net, but it was hopelessly tangled in the hooks of dozens of Lazy Ikes and Dardevles. I ran to the next boat and the net I found was the size of a coffee filter.

"The net! Get the net!" Doc continued.

In a blind panic, I jumped into the third boat and picked up the net. The frame was normal, but instead of only three feet of woven poly, 20 or 30 feet of net dragged behind me. I gathered as much as I could into my arms and tried to carry it toward struggling Doc, but it snagged on every bush and rock on the way, getting heavier and heavier as my strength waned.

A quick look toward the lake revealed Doc straining against the load on his line. "Hurry! The net!" he wailed.

Even though I pulled as hard as I could, I had too much net to drag. But no matter, because suddenly Doc's rod suddenly snapped upright, limp line dangling from the tip. Judy had broken off.

Exhausted, I fell to my knees and rolled over on my back, with yards of net wrapped around my neck and chest. Gripping the smooth rock, I closed my eyes to rest. As I took a few deep breaths to calm my racing heart, I began to gag on an impossibly foul odor. I tried to sit up, but Doc had me pinned to the ground, his smoldering cigar under my nose.

"Make me lose my dream fish, will you?" he growled, as he brought the cigar even closer.

I managed to grab his arm. And opening my eyes, through a bright light I saw Doc holding a capsule of smelling salts.

"You okay?" Doc asked with a broad smile.

"I guess so," I said. "How long have I been out?"

"Long enough," Doc answered. "Now that your tooth is fixed, you'll be able to pig out like crazy in the Bush."

Still a little groggy, I said, "Sorry you lost her, Doc."

"Don't worry about it," he said. "I'll be able to find another dental tech."

"Sure," I said, confusion giving way to the growing pain in my jaw. "But before you hire one, you better explain Judy to her."

"Good advice," Doc said thoughtfully. "It takes a special kind of woman to understand about Judy. Maybe a redhead."

I untied the slobber bib, climbed from the chair, and stretched my legs. I walked over to a photo of our fishing group taken many years ago. Our eyes were wide with excitement. I could hardly wait until the float plane carried us north again for another dream come true. And I said,

"Thanks, Doc."

EPISODE 23

For Some Fishermen, Trolling Is The End Of The Line

As far as Doc is concerned, trolling is for slugs on the sidewalk of life. He ranks trolling right up there with his least favorite things, which include babies screaming at bowling alleys, politicians voting themselves pay raises, and anyone performing rap music.

Doc said he looked up the word in the dictionary. Trolling derives from the Norwegian "troll," which refers to a person who drags a lure behind a moving boat instead of jigging straight up and down like civilized fishermen. The troll lives in caves or under bridges, frightens little children, and cheers for the Yankees. That description, according to Doc, matches me and a couple members of our group to a T. The T stands for "troll," of course.

Doc's aversion to trolling is nearly equaled by his dislike for gripping a vibrating outboard tiller six or eight hours a day, so I always get to drive when we share a boat, although we never go anywhere. Doc prefers to sit dead still, or move with a slight drift, smoke hideous cigars, and lift his jig up and down a foot off the bottom, up and down all day long. So I was somewhat surprised a few years ago when I joined him at a tackle shop to prepare for our annual Canadian fly-in and saw him put a giant spoon in his shopping cart.

"What are you going to do with that thing?" I asked.

"I read where jigging big spoons in deep water is becoming popular," Doc said, sheepishly.

"What are you going to use for tackle?" I asked, "a tent pole and telephone wire?" I knew he didn't own a rig big enough to haul that lure out of the water.

"No, probably a broomstick and clothesline rope," he said, a little irritation showing in his voice. It was easy to get Doc's goat by making fun of his fishing techniques, so I kept up the pressure.

"Say, there's a nice jigging rig, Doc," I taunted. He had picked up a five-ounce spinner unit with tandem chartreuse blades and a hook big enough to hang half a beef on. "Now I know where Captain Hook buys his extra prostheses," I said.

"Okay," Doc said. "You got me. I decided just this once, just this year, I'm going to try trolling to discover what you guys see in it."

I was so stunned you could have knocked me over with a marabou feather, but I said, "What we see in it, Doc, is fish."

"But how can you just sit and wait for a pike or walleye to hook itself?"

"There's a little more to it than that, Doc," I said, patiently. "Sometimes they put up a little bit of a fight."

"But trolling doesn't have the finesse or involve the expertise of presenting a jig," Doc said, moving his wrist up and down, up and down.

"I disrespectfully disagree, Doc," I said. "Trolling success depends on choosing the right lure and color, maintaining the right speed and depth, and working the rod to give it more action. It also takes some fancy helmsmanship to round the points and hug the weedbeds without running aground or getting snagged."

"And you cover about 80 nautical miles a day," Doc said, rubbing his lower back in anticipation.

"But you also get to outrun most of the bugs," I assured him.

As Doc moved on down the aisle, he chose a few more spoons and a family-size can of bug dope. "Just in case," he said. When he headed for the heavy-duty rods and reels, I knew he was serious about trolling.

A month later we stood on the dock of the only cabin on Wesleyan Lake. Back in Sioux Lookout, Knobby Clark had given us maps with likely hot spots for walleyes and pike. After well over 20 years flying into and fishing Northwest Ontario lakes, Knobby certainly knew what he was talking about.

Dale, Knobby's son-in-law, had flown us into the Bush. He told us what the previous fly-in party used to catch their biggest fish.

Doc held up his monster chartreuse spinner and asked, "Think they'll like this one?"

"Could be," Dale said. "But it's still early in the season, so you may do better with small to medium spoons. Dardevles. Red-and-whites are good. Also Five-of-Diamonds, Doctors, Ruby-Eyes, Professors, that sort of thing. Some crankbaits and Rapalas. Not many reeds or weeds growing yet, so try the points and fallen trees. Troll fairly fast. Good luck."

Dale taxied the blue Beaver back into the lake and prepared for take-off. It was a warm afternoon, and the six of us stood in the prop wash, enjoying the cool spray until the plane turned into the wind.

Fifteen minutes later, we were rigged

and ready to fish. "Want to drive, Doc?" I asked.

He gritted his teeth and said, "Naaah, not yet. It's enough that I'm prepared to troll. Running the engine would be sensory overload."

So we climbed on board and Doc watched carefully as I started the engine and headed toward the nearest point, about 50 yards from the cabin. I tossed a Big Doctor into the drink, let out 30 feet of line and made sure the drag was snug, but not too tight. The little Merc purred along quietly. I chose a speed I guessed at somewhere under 55 and prepared to catch my first fish of the trip.

Eyes not leaving my rod tip for a second, Doc ripped open the Velcro flap of his life vest pocket and pulled out a green cigar. I lived in a rental house once that had shag carpet the same color. When Doc lit up, the smoke rushed by me like a poltergeist with really bad body odor.

I realized the only thing that would suppress my gag reflex was catching a fish, and thankfully it happened. A good one, too. In one fluid motion I set the hook, jerked the tiller sideways, goosed the throttle to run the boat away from shore, cut the throttle, and put the engine in neutral.

Standing, I fought my catch to the boat. It was a nice pike, especially for my first fish, and it made two runs, the first with a back flip and a huge splash, before I could get a net under him. About five-and-a-half pounds, I guessed. The treble hook came out easy, and when I released him, he took off like a slimy shot.

Engine in gear, lure over the side, boat back up to speed, drag checked, and I was on another troll. I looked up and Doc was incredulous. At least I think that's the right word. It's from the Old English "incredudoc" and describes a dentist who witnesses an occurrence so unbelievable he lets his cigar go out.

"That was a nice fish, huh, Doc?" I asked.

"Mumble, mumble, mumble."

"You going to try it?" I couldn't wait for an answer because I had another fish on. I did what I had to and boated a two-pound ax-handle pike. This one didn't jump or run or get excited until I brought it on board. Then it knocked over Doc's can of bubbly and spit up something that looked either like a partially digested sucker or one of Doc's cigars.

Not to be outdone, Doc spit up his cigar, too. Then he grabbed his rod and said, "Let's troll!"

In only a few hours we caught and released maybe 60 fish, 10 of them walleyes and the rest pike. Doc was amazed at the fight from even the smallest pike.

In only a few hours we caught and released maybe 60 fish, 10 of them walleyes and the rest pike.

"They're more aggressive than I thought they'd be," Doc observed, unhooking a walleye that weighed less than his spoon. "It must be the wiggling, flashing target that gets them fired up."

We cleared a point where we picked up a double, two three-pound pike that could have been twins. Doc was finally beginning to smile. Maybe trolling wasn't so bad, after all.

Awhile later, Doc let out a whoop as he set the hook along a steep rock wall. I reeled in and positioned the boat so he could fight Mr. Big, a walleye caught on a fast-moving Ruby-Eye. The De-Liar said six pounds, which was all right with Doc. After a few snapshots, it swam back home, straight down through the cold brown water.

The next day we awakened to a fishing-prohibitive downpour. Doc spent the better part of the morning lecturing us on the finer points of trolling. While we all had known the pleasures of the technique for quite some time, Doc insisted he had some insights we somehow managed to miss. He wasted no time telling us the best ways to refine our moving presentation to make it more productive.

Full of all the expert advice they could stand, the boys overreacted. The banker said, "Doc, you're making way too much of this. Trolling is like plowing a field and every now and then hitting a rock."

The attorney said, "Trolling is about as exciting as watching golf on TV."

"I'd rather go to the mall with my mother-in-law," the plant manager said.

"It's like mowing your yard and every fourth or fifth round running over poop left by your neighbor's dog," the policeman said.

"On the contrary," Doc said. "Trolling is an exact science, a test of man and machine. Trolling is the Indy 500 of fishing methods. While you may not always get the checkered flag, you don't spend much time in the pits, either."

"Then where does that leave jigging?" I asked, afraid of the answer I'd get.

"Compared to trolling," Doc said, "jigging is like bobbing for apples."

A day or two later, we were in a walleye hole below a rapids. Distasteful as it was to Doc, we were jigging to fill our stringer for supper. As luck would have it, Doc landed a 17-pound pike on super-light tackle. After the fight and the photos and watching it swim away, Doc lit up a green skanker, leaned back, and said, "I don't believe I've ever caught such a nice apple."

On the spot, he said the experience put him off trolling for good. At first I thought he might be kidding. But then he said, "Here, I won't be needing these anymore," and he handed me about $65 worth of trolling lures.

As I gratefully wedged them into my already stuffed tackle box, all I could think of to say to my fickle friend was,

"Thanks, Doc."

> "Compared to trolling," Doc said, "jigging is like bobbing for apples."

EPISODE 24

A Fish In The Net Is Worth Two In The Lake

I was standing in a supermarket check-out line some time ago when this tabloid headline poked me in the eye: Aliens Ruin Fishfest! Since Doc and the rest of us compete in a small-scale big-fish contest each year in Canada, the story had particular significance, so I let my half gallon of rocky road liquefy while I read it.

It seems creatures that looked like Willie Nelson (an actual photo) had hovered their spaceship over a lake somewhere in Missouri and used a beam to transport schools of bass to an all-you-can-eat fish fry joint in Kansas City. A tournament scheduled for the lake was canceled. Anonymous authorities were investigating.

Weird as it was, I had every intention of putting the story

to good use. In past years I blamed the weather or my tackle or my bait or my bad luck for preventing me from landing a contest winner. Now I would add aliens to the list.

A week after my tabloid experience, we arrived at Knobby's for the annual fly-in. Knobby's wife Bobbie and his daughter Donna were making sure we all had licenses. New regulations had just taken effect that limited the number of large walleye and northern pike we could possess or take home. Donna explained that it was a good way to promote catch-and-release and would someday result in more trophy fish.

"You won't have to worry about him," Doc said, aiming his unlighted ball bat of a cigar in my direction. "Since we're each throwing five bucks into our big fish contest, I doubt he'll catch anything we need to measure."

I gave Doc a #7 dirty look, but deep down I knew he was right. For some reason, I can hook more than my share of hogs when it's only for fun. But with money to be lost, I may as well be dragging a Lindy Rig through dishwater.

Seven of us went on the trip that year. The banker's brother-in-law had joined us for a one-time adventure, probably sent as a spy to report what really goes on in the Bush. We unloaded two pickups and a van, and Knobby said it looked like we had enough tackle and provisions for a party of 16 for a month. Reluctantly, we left behind some extra coolers, a pool table, and a hot tub, but two Beavers and a Cessna 206 were still needed to lift us all onto Road House Lake.

Gear and food stowed, rods rigged, and engines gassed up, we motored away from the brand spanking new cabin to plumb the depths for dinner, and maybe capture the big-fish prize.

Doc insisted he and I share a boat the first day or two,

and that I drive. I thought it was probably because running the engine would interfere with his smoking habit. As if reading my mind, Doc wrestled another pond-scum-green cigar out of its box. I increased boat speed to create a Bic-snuffing wind, but he managed to light the thing anyway. The smoke reeked of sun-rotted chicken skin, but Doc didn't seem to notice as he tossed over the side a giant 10-inch floating blue Rapala rigged to a baitwalker. I trolled my yellow and orange silver-backed Five of Diamonds parallel to a massive wall that soared fast and steep from a rocky ledge 30 feet below.

In all the years we'd flown into Knobby's lakes on the Cat River chain, we had never quite figured out how to fish the rock walls. Sometimes drifting a jig tipped with a minnow or crawler was the only producer. At other times, anything with a hook worked if it was trolled fast enough. But even then, we never knew for sure how deep to fish or what we'd catch. The only species we ever boated in this area were northerns and walleyes, so we figured the chance was 50-50 that we'd pull in one or the other.

I jabbed the fish alarm feature on the portable sonar unit and it began to beep as if we were floating in the barracuda tank at the Shedd Aquarium in Chicago.

> Doc puffed on his cigar, sending an obscene smoke signal into the virgin air.

"Any fish down there?" Doc asked over the beep! beep! beep!

"Only a few dozen," I said, punching a button to kill the audio.

Two seconds later, Doc gave his heavy spincast rod a two-fisted yank and began to reel in what we both hoped was a reasonable fish. With every revolution of the handle, Doc puffed on his cigar, sending an obscene smoke signal into the virgin air. After a dozen cranks, instead of quickly rising to the surface, the uncooperative fish stayed down. Doc moaned, "It's a walleye. It's Mr. Big."

Doc's cigar rhythmically belched smoke, like The Little Engine Who Could as it chugged up the storybook mountain. "Get the net!" he whispered hoarsely.

"What for, Doc?" I asked. "You haven't pried him off the bottom yet."

In response, Doc gave the drag adjustment another click and cranked even harder. After what seemed like several minutes, the ghostly outline of a huge fish came into view. It was still too far under the surface for us to be sure what it was, but it had fins and wanted to fight.

> **The drag howled like a Jimi Hendrix guitar solo.**

Then it was gone as the drag spit out a string of zzzzzzzzzz's. Doc and the fish were right back where they'd started.

Another click on the drag adjustment and Doc tried to raise the fish again. As hard as he worked, you'd have thought he was winching in a 1949 Studebaker pickup full of firewood.

"Come on, big guy," Doc pleaded, a mass of gray smoke circling his head like a concrete halo. "Give it up, Mr. Big."

A dozen more revolutions and the writhing shadow appeared again, then dived almost straight down, taking Doc's rod tip a yard underwater. The drag howled like a Jimi Hendrix guitar solo.

To help Doc in his struggle, I had reeled in my line and slowly maneuvered the boat away from shore, in case we needed more room to operate. The LCD read 48 feet, and the bottom dropped off fast.

When Doc's drag stopped screaming, I figured the fish had returned to its ground floor apartment. Doc's arms were beginning to have muscle spasms, but he pulled and cranked, smoked and wheezed, while I coughed and gagged. The putrefied cloud of cigar smoke grew so dense that I could barely make out trees on the shore a mere 50 feet away.

I didn't know how much longer I could stand it, so I said, "I can't last through another run, Doc. Bring him up again and I'll have the net ready."

The reel was loaded with 17-pound mono. A 30-inch 25-pound steel leader with a cross-lock snap connected the Rapala to the bottom walker. And Doc had me tie a flawless terminal knot, so the fish wasn't going to escape.

A Niagara Falls of sweat ran down Doc's forehead, and he groaned like a galley slave rowing at ramming speed. "I see it!" Doc yelled.

I took a peek over the side at the water swirling about six feet from the boat. I still couldn't identify the monster's species because it was too far away and the dark water was beginning to boil with every muscular flick of its fins.

"Closer, Doc!" I urged. "Bring it closer to the boat so I can get the net on him!"

Even though Doc was near exhaustion, he managed to keep the line tight. His hands were all cranked out, so he lifted the rod to head level and pulled like a Clydesdale. Then it happened. The end of Doc's cigar, glowing white hot from his constant puffing, brushed the mono, and the line parted like a meat cleaver slicing through a strand of overcooked spaghetti.

With the pressure suddenly released, a weakened Doc sat down hard on the boat seat. The shock dislodged his cigar, which landed in his open tackle box and began eating a bag of plastic grubs. I watched, fascinated, as it burned through a $6.95 lure or two and continued south. I thought of Jack Lemmon in The China Syndrome and wondered if the aluminum boat bottom would stop Doc's cigar butt meltdown.

Then, suddenly, from the corner of my eye, I caught a movement in the water. I took a swipe with the net and brought a thrashing mass of fish flesh into the boat.

The controversy continues to this day. I'll concede that Doc hooked the fish. But since I was the one to actually catch the fish—two walleyes, a 6-pounder and a 4-pounder, on the same Rapala—I claimed them as my own. Out of the goodness of my heart and spirit of fair play, I did return Doc's lure, however.

The 6-pounder became the big-fish contest winner in the walleye category that year, and he and his smaller hookmate are probably still swimming around Road House Lake, telling their side of the story.

On the downside, the event subjected Doc to major heckling from the rest of the guys. He also had to invest in a new tackle box.

When friends who have heard the tale ask how I finally won a big-fish contest after so many years, I tell them it wasn't the weather or my tackle or my bait choice. It was an alien who looked a lot like my dentist.

Thanks, Doc.

EPISODE 25

Potty Talk

Back when Moses was in Pampers, a story made the circuit about a man who came upon a friend breaking a long branch off a tree.

"What are you doing?" the man asked his friend.

"I dropped my coat down the hole in the outhouse," his friend said, "and I need the stick to fish it out."

Revolted, the man said, "Your coat's ruined! Just leave it there."

To which his friend replied, "I would, but my lunch is in the pocket."

I'm sure we've all heard our share of the dozens of anecdotes similar to this one, whether we wanted to or not. Those of us who have used primitive remote facilities know a thing or two about short-term physical and olfactory discomfort. But while some of us aren't overly inconvenienced when performing normal bodily functions in these odious commodes, others go to great lengths, transforming the experience into a ritual.

Those of us who have used primitive remote facilities know a thing or two about short-term physical and olfactory discomfort.

At about the halfway point on our long drive to Knobby Clark's at Sioux Lookout, Ontario, we like to take a break and stretch our legs at a combination convenience store and gas station in Cloquet, Minnesota. Creatures of bad habits, we've done this every year since our annual drive-up fly-in trips began over 20 years ago.

One year, much like the others, the plant manager and I topped off the gas tanks for the run to the border while Doc and the others went inside to scope the racks of reading material. Actually, not much reading is involved, unless photo captions are considered a form of literature. The captions usually tend toward, "My name is Buffy, and my favorite thing is doing volunteer work at the nursing home. I like strong, sensitive men who aren't afraid to cry. After college I'm going to be an actress, get married, have a lot of kids, and when I'm 26, retire to a Colorado condo." Oh, sure. And I'm going to quit my job, move to Arizona, and write a column for a fishing magazine. Who do they think they're kidding?

Anyway, a few of the guys in the group buy these, uh, picture books, for what they say is good reason. They think they can't have a successful, um, stay in the outhouse unless they have something, uh, distracting to take their minds off the spiders and buzzing insects.

As for other essential W.C. accessories, Doc had often said he'd rather replace the Charmin with splintery pine bark than do without his cigar, and I had no reason to doubt his sincerity. Also, as Doc explains, when he's ensconced on the throne, the smoke boiling up from his eye-watering stogie makes it almost impossible to see words on a page, so he prefers to squint at pictures, some of which fold out to billboard size.

I paid for the gas and glanced up as Doc picked up a magazine with the cover photo of a girl riding a motorcycle. At 55 miles per hour, her clothing wouldn't stop many June bugs, if you get my drift.

"Does it have to be that kind of book?" I asked.

"Well," Doc answered, "due to our change in diet and the unusual pressures of this trip, I find I need an extra strong stimulus in addition to a good cigar, to relax my plumbing."

I gave some thought to what Doc considered a good cigar, and a gaggle of goose bumps toured my stomach lining. "So you don't have stuff like this in your house?" I choked.

"Nope," Doc said. "To maintain our loving relationship, my wife has two rules. The first is no cigars in the bathroom."

"And number two?" (Maybe not a good phrase here.)

"No magazines. She thinks it's tacky."

"Then what do you do in the privacy of your own privy?"

"Sometimes I dig around under the sink and read labels on cleaning products."

"You're kidding."

"No," Doc said, "I'm not. Do you know that the scrubbing bubbles in Dow Bathroom Cleaner contain n-Alkyl dimethyl benzyl ammonium chlorides?"

This revelation made me see Doc in a new light. A dim bulb came to mind. "So you don't have anything else to read?" I asked.

"Occasionally the newspaper," Doc said, "but I usually

use the facilities at my office where I can enjoy a cigar and relax with what I choose."

"I'll bet your patients appreciate that." I imagined a haze of cigar smoke floating through Doc's dental office waiting room, and little Johnny in for his check-up asking, "Mommy, why is the lady in the magazine dressed like the Easter Bunny?"

Guessing my thoughts, Doc said, "I had an extra heavy duty exhaust fan installed, and I keep the magazines locked up with the Novocain." (Obviously a hidden meaning here.)

While I can understand wanting to make visits to the potty reasonably enjoyable, I don't like to spend an inordinate amount of time there, especially if I'm sharing a deep woods loo with a bunch of fishermen who are on a week-long binge of onions, fried eggs, pork and beans, and malt beverages that should carry the surgeon general's warning about the danger of supersonic flatulence.

And even more so if the facility is a two-holer located in the middle of a mosquito factory, separated from an outpost cabin by 150 feet of jagged rocks, tree roots, and thorny foliage.

Doc and the policeman carried several books to the counter and coughed up $14.60.

"Wouldn't Exlax be cheaper?" I asked.

Doc gave me a constipated frown, stuffed the books into a plain brown wrapper, and headed for the car to complete the trip to Knobby's and the fly-in.

Days later, after bouncing around on a boat seat 10 hours a day, inhaling a bag or three of vinegar potato chips, and drinking coffee with the consistency and flavor of 90-weight gear oil, regularity took a hike. In the morning when we loaded the boats, the conversation went something like: "Got the net?" "Check." "Crawlers?" "Check." "All gassed up?" "Oh, man." "Toilet tissue?" "Two rolls." "Let's go fishing."

One early afternoon, Doc and I were yanking entire schools of three-pound walleyes out of a narrow corridor along a rock wall. A steady breeze blew from left to right, and we agreed we'd never had such a perfect drift. Between catches, Doc lit a cigar that looked like the giant bratwurst served at the Red Frog in Cedar Rapids. Except it was the color of moldy alfalfa, with a corresponding odor. I was upwind of the stench, so my fishing enjoyment was not the least bit compromised.

Suddenly a weird look crossed Doc's face, and he said, "Want to pull into shore after the next fish?"

"Gotta go?" I asked.

Doc chewed his bale of hay, nodded and replied, "Ummph."

I was the engine man that day. He was at my mercy. I took the opportunity to leisurely exchange a chartreuse for a purple plastic grub. Before I dropped it over the side, I rummaged through the cooler for a bubbly, which I popped and took a sip or two. Then I rearranged my seat cushion and stretched.

Doc said, "Ooomaah," and began to sweat.

Maybe purple wasn't right after all, so I opened my tackle box and pulled out five or six other colors and held them underwater one at a time, to see how they looked.

Doc's knuckles were white as he gripped the sides of the boat. I noticed that his cigar had gone out.

Sensing his discomfort reaching critical mass, I said, "You know, Doc, we picked up a couple good northerns along here. Why don't we put on some spoons and troll down to the rapids? I'll bet it won't take 20 or 30 minutes..."

Dead cigar bit almost in two, Doc looked like he was holding his breath. Then he mumbled...

"What?" I asked.

He mumbled something else from the pointy end of the 14-foot Lund.

"Want to troll awhile?" I asked again.

What Doc yelled at me wasn't exactly, "Run for the beach!" but I got the idea, so I started up the little Merc and made a full throttle dash for shore. The closest spot was a typical Northwest Ontario cove with reeds and a high-water line of ice-out logs, then a tangle of bushes and dark trees beyond. As I cut and tilted the engine, I turned to see Doc leaping and splashing through the final 20 feet of shallow water—life vest suddenly flung to the side with one hand while he yanked at his belt with the other.

I catch a lot of nature shows on big-screen TV. I especially enjoy watching bull moose destroy trees during the rut. When I crank up the volume, shows in stereo are almost like being there. But I've never in my life seen or heard anything like Doc plowing his way through the reeds, leaping over logs, and crashing through underbrush—a mad stampede inland, raising clouds of voracious mosquitoes with every step.

After clearing the briar patch, he was out of sight, but still stumbling another few yards into the woods. Then quiet. In the meantime, I used an oar to retrieve his life vest, then pushed off and selected a spot that would be easier for his return. I also hooked and released a few scrappy northerns in the reeds as I waited.

Finally, Doc appeared. I expected him to be all smiles when I picked him up, but he wasn't. We fished some more and he smoked another moldy gagger, and at sundown we headed silently for the cabin.

After an outstanding meal of baked walleye with onions flambeaux, I was being soundly thrashed by the attorney at cribbage. Doc sat down gingerly beside me. "I need some help," he said, sheepishly.

Since that was the first time I had ever heard Doc ask for help from anyone, anywhere, and since my cribbage hand looked like a foot, I said, "Shoot."

"Remember when I told you I'd rather give up the Charmin than do without my cigar?" Doc said.

"Yes," I said.

"Well, this afternoon in the woods was obviously an emergency situation."

"What are you trying to tell me, Doc?"

"I had my cigar, all right, but I forgot the Charmin in the boat."

"You didn't."

"I did. And the only thing within reach was pine bark."

"You didn't."

"I did," Doc confessed. "And I think a few splinters got stuck in my, uh, right cheek."

> The memory of Doc bent over the dining room table, his injured area illuminated by a Coleman lantern, still brings tears to my eyes.

The attorney, never one to let a buddy's misfortune pass unridiculed, gathered the rest of the group and retold the story in minute detail—how Doc had managed to get sharp parts of the Bush lodged in his tush.

Revolting as it was, a minor operation was called for, and we cut cards to see who would be head surgeon. I lost. While I went to the sink to scrub, the policeman flame-sterilized the tweezers and, to Doc's horror, a fillet knife. The banker administered anesthesia from a bottle of Old Overshoe.

The memory of Doc bent over the dining room table, his injured area illuminated by a Coleman lantern, still brings tears to my eyes. Each time the tweezers removed a splinter, Doc yelped with pain and we howled with laughter. The surgery over, the plant manager poured on a quart or so of hydrogen peroxide to prevent infection, after which Doc jumped up and trotted around the room, whinnying like a horse with a burr under its saddle—which wasn't far from the truth.

Over the years, Doc has been a wellspring of knowledge, a protector of the environment, a brilliant fisherman, and on occasion, a complete jerk. But he's also a forgiving friend and a good sport, even when he's been the butt of a joke.

Thanks, Doc.

ABOUT THE AUTHOR

Greg Knowles, born on a ping-pong table in the basement of his parents' home near Knoxville, Iowa, hasn't stopped bouncing around since. After a four-year naval career and an Iowa State journalism degree, he did hard time at Midwest advertising agencies. He's currently a freelance writer and creative consultant in Mesa, Arizona, where he shares his life with his wife Sandy Tweedy and an assortment of fishing tackle and friends.

IN-FISHERMAN MASTERPIECE SERIES

- **WALLEYE WISDOM:** A Handbook of Strategies
- **BASS:** A Handbook of Strategies
- **PIKE:** A Handbook of Strategies
- **SMALLMOUTH BASS:** A Handbook of Strategies
- **CRAPPIE WISDOM:** A Handbook of Strategies
- **CHANNEL CATFISH FEVER:** A Handbook of Strategies
- **LARGEMOUTH BASS IN THE 1990s:** A Handbook of Strategies

Each masterpiece book represents the collaborative effort of fishing experts. The books don't represent a regional perspective or the opinions of one good angler. Each masterpiece book is species specific, but teems with information applicable to all areas of the country and to any fishing situation.

IN-FISHERMAN LIBRARY SERIES
Up-to-date Information from Individual Angling Authorities.

FISHING FUNDAMENTALS
Wade Bourne goes back to angling basics. He explains how to select tackle and lures, how to find hot fishing spots, how to fight and land fish, and even how to clean and cook the catch.

An excellent book for beginners or a review for anyone who fishes.

ICE FISHING SECRETS
Al Lindner, Doug Stange, and Dave Genz talk tactics and strategies for ice fishing today. They cover equipment trends, rigging breakthroughs, seasonal fish locations, and proper presentations. Species by species coverage includes walleyes, pike, perch, bluegills, crappies, trout, largemouth bass, smallmouth bass, and more.

In-Fisherman
COMMUNICATIONS NETWORK

The **In-Fisherman Library Series** is but part of the In-Fisherman Communications Network, a multifaceted, multimedia organization, teaching how to catch fish while striving to maintain a healthy fishing resource for future generations.

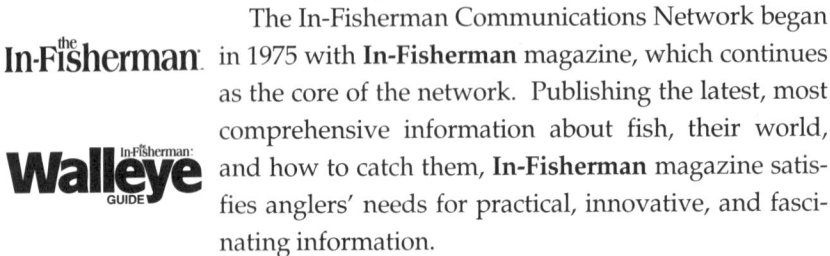

The In-Fisherman Communications Network began in 1975 with **In-Fisherman** magazine, which continues as the core of the network. Publishing the latest, most comprehensive information about fish, their world, and how to catch them, **In-Fisherman** magazine satisfies anglers' needs for practical, innovative, and fascinating information.

In addition to **In-Fisherman** magazine and the **In-Fisherman Library Series,** the In-Fisherman Communications Network publishes the **In-Fisherman Masterpiece Book Series,** species-specific books representing the collaborative effort of several fishing experts; and the **Walleye Guide** and **Walleye In-Sider** magazines—North America's leading sources for walleye information.

And that's only print media. **In-Fisherman TV Specials** are hailed as the most informative fishing shows on television. **In-Fisherman Radio** plays on 850 stations nationwide, reaching over a billion listeners annually. **In-Fisherman Video Club** presents a treasury of angling wisdom on a variety of fish species from a large library of videos, with 6 to 8 new releases each year. The **Professional Walleye Trail** pits the world's best walleye anglers in run-and-gun fishing competition across North America.

For information on any area of the In-Fisherman Communications Network, write In-Fisherman Inc., Two In-Fisherman Dr., Brainerd, MN 56401, 218/829-1648.

In-Fisherman Video
In-Fisherman Television
In-Fisherman Radio